ARIEL DORFMAN

KONFIDENZ

Ariel Dorfman, born in Argentina in 1942, is a Chilean citizen who was forced into exile after the 1973 coup that overthrew Salvador Allende. He is the author of numerous novels, plays, and essays, including *The Empire's Old Clothes*, *Mascara*, *The Last Song of Manuel Sendero*, and *Widows*. His award-winning play, *Death and the Maiden*, was made into a film by Roman Polanski. He lives with his family in Durham, North Carolina.

INTERNATIONAL

Acclaim for **ARIEL DORFMAN's**

KONFIDENZ

"Hypnotic and harrowing . . . Dostoyevskian in intensity. . . . Dorfman explodes conventional writing technique to produce a work that tests the boundaries of contemporary fiction. *Konfidenz* is a house of mirrors, forcing readers to look within and question not only their own notions of political loyalty and ideals, but also truth and imagination, love and the very nature of trust. . . . An extraordinary story."

—*Washington Post Book World*

"The gifted and versatile Dorfman's new novel, written almost entirely in dialogue, develops an almost unbearable intensity. . . . A political novel as well as an acute study in character and obsession. . . . Exhilarating for its finely tuned unfolding but somber in its conclusions, *Konfidenz* demands a fundamental reexamination of the nature of trust."

—*Publishers Weekly*

"Lush, finely stylized, sensual . . . [Dorfman's] writing resides in the country of Beauty. . . . *Konfidenz* is Teflon-coated, a spy story where nothing sticks. . . . Questions catalyze further questions until the entire text becomes a chemical reaction, all afizz in possibilities both mystical and political."

—*Voice Literary Supplement*

Also by **ARIEL DORFMAN**

How to Read Donald Duck
(with Armand Mattelart)

The Empire's Old Clothes

Widows

The Last Song of Manuel Sendero

Mascara

Last Waltz in Santiago
and Other Poems of Exile and Disappearance

Hard Rain

My House Is on Fire

Some Write to the Future

Death and the Maiden

KONFIDENZ

ARIEL DORFMAN

VINTAGE INTERNATIONAL

VINTAGE BOOKS

A DIVISION OF RANDOM HOUSE, INC.

NEW YORK

FIRST VINTAGE INTERNATIONAL EDITION, JANUARY 1996

 Published in the United States by Vintage Books, a division of Random House, Inc., New York, and simultaneously in Canada by Random House of Canada, Limited, Toronto. Originally published in hardcover by Farrar, Straus and Giroux, New York, in 1995. This edition published by arrangement with Farrar, Straus and Giroux, Inc.

Library of Congress Cataloging-in-Publication Data
Dorfman, Ariel.
Konfidenz / Ariel Dorfman. — 1st Vintage International ed.
p. cm.
ISBN 0-679-76716-9
1. Refugees, Political—Fiction. I. Title.
PR9309.9.D67K66 1996
863—dc20 95-37600
CIP

Manufactured in the United States of America
10 9 8 7 6 5 4 3 2 1

This book is for Angélica.

She knows why.

The last word has not yet been said.

—Bertolt Brecht

I am a liar who always tells the truth.

—Jean Cocteau

KONFIDENZ

As soon as the woman enters room 242, the phone rings.

She does not answer immediately. She remains there in the doorway, her suitcase in one hand and the key in the other, examining the empty room, as if waiting for someone to appear out of nowhere and answer.

The phone rings again.

I see the woman hesitate for one more moment. Then, suddenly in a hurry, she lets the suitcase fall, crosses the room, and picks up the receiver. Before she can speak, she hears the voice of a man.

"Barbara?"

It's a voice the woman has never heard before.

"Who's this?"

"One of Martin's friends."

"That's a relief. I was beginning to get worried. Martin wasn't waiting for me at the . . ."

"But the chauffeur did come to . . ."

"Yes, but he didn't bring any message from Martin. He seemed deaf and dumb. And the truth—"

"The truth?"

"It seemed strange that Martin should send a limousine. Not exactly his style."

"I sent the limo, Barbara."

"Thanks, but you shouldn't have bothered."

"I wanted to make sure you had a smooth arrival, Barbara. Your departure must have been a bit difficult."

"It wasn't, well—easy."

"But you're here."

"My father has connections."

"So you shouldn't have trouble going back."

"Why should I have trouble?"

"Some people do."

"I don't expect any trouble whatsoever."

"I'm glad to hear that, for your sake. It's always good to be able to go back to one's own country."

"You're also from . . . ?"

"I thought you would have guessed by now."

"Are you?"

"Not anymore."

"Not anymore? Martin never told me he had a friend who . . ."

"A friend who—what?"

"A friend like you."

"You got letters from him?"

"He wrote a lot."

"And he never . . . ?"

"No."

"He probably had better things to write about."

If someone were watching her, it might seem that she hesitates, that she waits before answering. The pause, if it exists at all, lasts only for an instant. Then she says:

"What I'd like to know is why Martin didn't . . . ?"

"He couldn't make it to Paris today."

"Where is he?"

"On his way."

"And he asked you to take care of me?"

"Not exactly."

"So then why have you . . . ? When is he coming?"

"As soon as he can."

"Look, Mr. . . . Mr. . . . Excuse me, but I don't believe you told me your name."

"You can call me Leon."

"Does that mean your name isn't Leon?"

"It matters that much—what someone's called? Here in France, people call me Leon."

"Look, Mr. Leon, I—"

"Just Leon. No misters, please."

She does not answer right away. She has the feeling that someone is watching her. She turns. Through the half-open door, a maid who is pretending to clean up observes her.

"Can you hold on for a second . . . Leon?"

She goes to the door. The maid does not react. While her hand continues polishing a small marble table in the hallway, she stares into the room. Barbara doesn't say a thing. She brings the suitcase in and closes the door.

"Leon?"

"Something happened to you."

"A maid was looking at me through the door."

"Through the keyhole?"

"I'd left the door open when I—"

"The French can be extremely intrusive. Don't worry about it. They hate us because of—"

"I don't know what I'm doing in this hotel. Martin has an apartment."

"You were surprised when the chauffeur brought you to the hotel?"

"It is slightly—extravagant. But I thought Martin—well, he wanted someplace special to welcome me—you know . . ."

"Yes. Someplace romantic."

"Of course, a romance needs two participants, Leon, and as I see no sign of Martin—it might be better if I went to Martin's apartment to wait for him. Don't you think so?"

"And you know the address?"

"Not really. He asked me to write to a post office box, he told me—"

"That concierges in Paris can't be trusted with the mail, right?"

"Yes, that is what he wrote to me, in fact. But I know that it's in the rue des Canettes, his apartment, I mean. Of course you must know the address. Given that you seem to know so much about him."

"And what if Martin no longer lived there?"

"He didn't tell me he was moving."

"Moving is not the word I would use."

She waits for a moment. From a nearby church, a bell begins to peal. When it stops, all she can hear is the sudden agitated flapping of a pigeon's wings against her window. Finally, she speaks:

"Look, Leon, you don't have to go on pretending with me."

Something seems to change in the man's voice:

"What do you mean?"

"Something's happened to him. To Martin."

"Oh."

"So you really don't need to pretend any longer. I know that something's happened. That's why I came. I would never have come if I hadn't—I don't like to leave the—"

"The boys. Yes. Martin told me that you're working with those boys. Did you bring copies of the photos?"

"Some. Why are you asking?"

"Just wondering. I'd like to see what they see. The city as they—"

"They're very talented. I'm just worried whether they'll be able to manage until I—"

"I'm sure they'll manage without you."

"I don't think so. They need me. But when I got Martin's urgent note . . ."

"Life or death."

"Yes. That's what he wrote. Life or death. He's sick, isn't he? Martin, I mean, did he—did he have an accident?"

"Martin's fine. Healthwise, I mean."

"That's not true. He's in danger."

"What sort of danger?"

"We're living in dangerous times, Leon. Wouldn't you say?"

"And if war is declared, things will get more dangerous."

"So Martin . . ."

"I would prefer, for now, to say that Martin needs—let's say, help, he needs help, Barbara, and if we don't help him, then he could, in fact, be in danger. But not yet."

"Help him? Who?"

"You and I. I don't think Martin has anyone else in the world."

"I'm sorry, Leon, but this can't go on."

"What can't go on?"

"This. This conversation. I need to see your face if we are going to . . . I'm in room—"

"242. Yes. I know. I'm the one who fixed the hotel. And I'm also the one who sent you the ticket."

"Martin sent me the ticket."

"It was me."

"Who are you?"

"I already told you. Martin's friend. Someone you can trust."

"And why are we talking like this, then, without—? Unless . . . You have seen me, haven't you? You know who I am, right, what I look like?"

"I know you."

"I felt that there was—as soon as I arrived, I knew there was somebody else, somebody was watching me. And maybe more than one person."

"More than one person?"

"Watching me. So it was you?"

"I'm not going to lie to you. It was me."

"And why didn't you simply come up and introduce yourself if you were going to call me up anyway and—?"

"I'd rather not until you get to know me a little better. So you can understand that in order to save Martin—"

"Save him! But you just said that he wasn't in—"

"I said not yet. But if you don't cooperate, something dreadful can happen to him. Let me correct myself. Something dreadful will most certainly happen. There are people who—but we'll talk about that later."

"Martin has never got involved in—problems. Why would he . . . ?"

"I think you're overly excited, Barbara. I should have given you time to unpack your suitcase. You'll find your favorite perfume, soap, everything you need, in the bathroom. Take a shower, change clothes, and I'll give you a call in—let's say half an hour."

"No, no. Tell me now."

"I'll give you a call in half an hour."

"Wait. Don't hang up. How can I know you'll call me, how can I trust that—"

"You've heard my voice. You know about these things, about people. Is there anything in my voice that suggests I could harm you?"

"No."

"You really mean that?"

"Yes. There's something—special, in your voice."

"You can't know how happy that makes me. I'll call you in half an hour."

She hears a click and then the long, tenacious buzzing of the dialing signal. I see her remain like that for a while with the receiver close to her ear. Afterwards, she hangs up and lets her eyes roam around room 242. It is as empty as ever.

Someone is there.

Someone is watching them.

Trying to watch the woman in that room, trying to listen to the voice on the phone, someone else, someone with plans for them.

A man.

For now, this is all you can surmise about him: that he is male and that he has plans.

You listen to their words as if that man on the phone and that woman in that hotel lived outside your will, as if they would have existed somewhere—yes, but where?—even if you were not transcribing this text already written with their bodies. That is why, at times, the story simply flows from your fingers—as if it were not possible to make a mistake, as if you were no more than their faraway secretary, an accident, a mere intermediary. At other times . . .

You are not alone in this task.

That is when you feel the possibility, the remote breath of his presence, of that man watching. When you wonder what they have really said to each other over the phone, when their voices become muffled, and yet you are responsible for getting every word they say right, exactly what that man who calls himself Leon told that woman, what she answered, when each word begins to fade before it can be written down or even read, it is then you become aware of somebody else who also guesses at their conversation, tries to examine who they are, what they will be doing.

Of that somebody else, you know next to nothing. Not even his existence is certain at this stage. But this you do know: if he does exist, that man who tries to watch has no interest in writing their story.

He has other plans for them.

Almost before the telephone rings, she answers it.

"Barbara?"

"Yes."

"Are you comfortable?"

"Does it matter?"

"It does. I'd rather you weren't standing."

"How do you know I'm standing?"

"If you lay down on the bed, you'd feel better."

"I have no intention whatsoever of lying down on the bed. Or anywhere else for that matter."

"Please, Barbara. You know lying down will help you feel better. As long as you don't wrinkle your blue dress. There. Isn't that better?"

"Who told you about my blue dress?"

"Who do you think told me?"

"Martin? But he never cares about these—"

"You're not going to deny that blue is your favorite color, are you?"

"Can you hold on a minute?"

The woman stands up, goes to one of the windows, and looks out. Almost in front of her, clinging to the second story of the building on the other side of the street, a scaffolding rises. When she arrived at the hotel less than an hour ago, a crew of workers was noisily making repairs. Now they are no longer there. They must have gone on a coffee break. She closes the curtains vigorously. Room 242 darkens. A ray of light, so thin that it is almost nonexistent, filters between the curtains. I don't see her switching on the lamp. She picks up the receiver again. Before she speaks, she lies down once more against the soft pillows on the bed. Next to her I see a camera.

"I don't see why you're so interested in the color of my dress."

"It's always important to know how the person we're talking to is dressed."

"You know how I'm dressed, but I don't even know your name, your real name."

"I'm sorry. That's something I can't reveal. Just yet. Ask me something else."

"How old are you?"

"That depends."

"What do you mean—that depends?"

"That depends. Most people count their age from the day of their birth. I'm not like them. I began to really exist much later."

She doesn't say anything. He waits. Then his voice asks:

"Don't you want to know how many years later?"

"If you want to tell me . . ."

"Twelve. Something special happened to me when I was twelve."

"What was it?"

"I think you know something about children that age."

"Why should I?"

"As the children you work with are all around twelve years of age, I thought you'd understand that special things happen to boys at that age."

Again, they are both silent, each waiting for the other to start up the conversation. Finally, he is the one who speaks:

"Would it bother you if I asked you a question?"

"Why should it bother me?"

"It's just that I didn't want to offend you."

"I don't offend easily."

"Well, then—tell me something: when Martin used to call you the woman of his dreams, what did you feel?"

Unexpectedly, from outside, the sound of hammers starts up. The construction workers have returned. She waits for another moment, listening carefully for something else, and then:

"Martin never called—"

"Please, Barbara, we both know that Martin called you the woman of his dreams; probably other men did as well. Dream woman. Every man in the world has said those words to every woman. Just as they say to them: I could eat you up. Or to other men: Hey, man, I could have her for dessert. A sad metaphor for sex. And also a lie. Dead sounds. They have no real intention of eating the woman. Just like the poor guys have no idea what it really means to dream a woman. Barbara, are you listening to me?"

She doesn't answer. She seems to be waiting for him to continue, but his voice is silent. She plays with the lens on the camera, moving it back and forth sluggishly. After a long time, he speaks:

"Barbara?"

"Yes."

"Is something the matter?"

"Yes."

"What's the matter?"

"I'm scared."

"You shouldn't be."

"Look, Leon, or whatever your name is, the truth is that I'm in a—let's call it delicate—I'm in a delicate situation. I don't speak French—and my only contact in this country is a man who says he's Martin's friend but who offers no proof and who won't show me his face and won't tell me his real name. The truth is that I would return home tomorrow if it weren't that Martin told me it was urgent, that I shouldn't—"

"That you shouldn't tell anyone, that's right, that you should tell everyone that your final destination was Rome, I know exactly what Martin's message said."

"How come you know?"

"Because I read that letter. I've read all the letters."

"All of them?"

"All of them.

"What right did you have to—?"

"I'm in charge of him. It's what people in charge do."

"I don't understand."

"What is it you don't understand?"

"That you're in charge of—what are you in charge of?"

"Please, Barbara. You don't need to make believe you don't know. Not with me."

"I'm not making believe anything."

"You're right to make believe you don't know. And knowing, I mean really knowing, well, of course, you don't. But Martin himself commented that you suspected he wasn't coming to Paris to continue his architecture studies, that he was involved in—well, you know."

"I don't know what you're talking about."

"Come on, Barbara—you're not going to deny that before Martin went off you asked him if he had—other reasons for coming, those were the exact words: 'Barbara asked me if I wasn't going to France for other reasons.' You must have seen how ashamed he felt, because he couldn't tell you the truth. But that was our fault, I want you to know that he would have told you everything, except that it was expressly forbidden to inform any of you, his parents, his girlfriend, his friends, not one of you could know what he was really coming to do here."

"So what was he coming to do here?"

"You know."

"That's not true."

"What's not true?"

"I never asked Martin if he was going to France for—other reasons. We never talk about that sort of thing."

"What sort of thing?"

"Politics."

"And war?"

"There's not going to be a war."

"Oh, there's going to be a war."

"We try not to talk about that. And we steer clear of—politics."

"Then why did Martin tell me that you brought up your suspicions before he left?"

"It must have been to impress you, so you wouldn't think that he wanted to marry a woman who didn't agree with his—but this is an absurd conversation. If what you're telling me about Martin were true, you wouldn't be announcing it like this, on the phone, to someone you don't even know."

"First of all, I don't feel that you are somebody I don't know. I have total trust in your—"

"That's nice to know. I can't tell you how thrilled I am that you—"

"Please. Sarcasm doesn't suit you."

"Something else Martin told you about me?"

"The second thing I wanted to say: your hotel prizes itself on ensuring the privacy of its guests. So nobody can hear us."

"I don't believe you."

"Look, we know our business. Martin's safety is our primary concern—so you'll know I'm—listen, I'm the only one who knows Martin's real name in Paris. The others have always known him as Hans. They've never even seen him."

"Hans?"

"His underground name."

"This conversation is getting dangerous."

"Strange. Martin told me that you were a woman without fear. What you're doing with those kids, for instance, even if your father is protecting you—giving them the liberty to take any photograph they want in the midst of the paranoia that we—Martin told me that you like danger, that at times you take unnecessary risks only to see if you can live through them without the rhythm of your heart rising."

"He can't have—Martin would never talk about me with a stranger, telling him intimate things."

"Martin told me everything about you, Barbara."

"What things?"

"Things about you. Things only he knew."

"What things?"

"About your body."

"What did he tell you about my body?"

"Your breasts."

"You're making this up."

"You don't use a bra. You like to feel the blouse against your nipples. But you'd rather not have your blouse on at all."

"What else did he tell you?"

"How warm your breasts are. As if they had just been in the sun. Even on a cold day."

"What else?"

"Your clitoris. You don't like a man's fingers on your clitoris."

"Son of a bitch."

She puts the phone down and goes to the mirror on the other side of the room. She looks for her own face in the mirror, she looks for her eyes, she breathes deeply and then crosses the carpet, back to the bed, back to the phone. For a moment, someone observing her might speculate that she is about to hang up. She does not.

"What a son of a bitch."

"If you have to blame somebody, Barbara, blame us. We forced him. Not only Martin. All of them. Security reasons."

"And who else did he tell about my . . . ?"

"Nobody else. He only told me because Willy was—"

"Who's Willy?"

"The man who should have been in charge of Martin here in Paris. He's my closest friend. Shows how precarious human existence is. If Willy hadn't come down with pneumonia, I wouldn't even know the color of Martin's eyes, let alone his real name, and you wouldn't be here and Martin wouldn't have anybody to save him . . . But Willy was hospitalized in Marmottan at six in the morning the very day Martin was arriving from—and by eight Wolf had—"

"That's his real name?"

"I don't know his real name. By eight Wolf had called me to replace Willy. It was urgent, he said, because a man named Hans was arriving a couple of hours later from home. I had to accept, though I'd been in charge of the last two and was already overworked.

"What sort of work do you do?"

"I used to work for a newspaper back home."

"Which one?"

"They closed it six years ago. You wouldn't know it. You were too young when they—"

"Don't be so sure. There was a newspaper on the other side of the street from my school and then they—"

"I really don't like to talk about this, Barbara."

"I understand."

"I speak French very well, almost perfectly, but the authorities here won't let me work as a journalist, so I get some money for doing research on evidence about Hebrew nuptial rites in the Old Testament."

"You're Jewish?"

"No. Do I sound Jewish?"

"Just a question. Otherwise, I don't understand who would pay you in order to . . ."

"It's a front. Phony research. I don't really study that. The people who put up the money know that I'm really engaged in other—activities—though they don't know exactly what—I mean, they don't know that men like Martin come through Paris and— Anyway, it's not enough. If it weren't that Claudia manages to—"

"Claudia?"

"My wife."

"You're married?"

"Is it a relief to know that I'm married?"

"The truth is, yes."

"Because you don't trust me."

"What do you want me to say?"

"I always want you to tell me the truth."

"Well, then, yes. I don't trust you."

"You think I'm trying to get information from you about Martin, trying to get you to admit that you're also interested in politics?"

"I already told you—I have no idea what you're trying to do or who you are. For that matter, I'm not even sure that you've ever met Martin—or if that woman you mentioned—Claudia?—if she exists at all."

"Believe me that it's lucky for all of us that she exists."

"And how does she make a living?"

"I'd rather not talk about that."

"And I'd rather end this conversation, then—as you're not answering any of my questions with straight answers, not one of the—"

"Sorry to interrupt you, but have you got your shoes on?"

"I don't see what that has—?"

"You seem tense. When your shoes press in too much, you get sort of nervous. What I mean is that if you take your shoes off and try to relax a bit, maybe—"

"You don't want me to be tense? Just stop talking to me about my clothes or the way I—because you don't know anything about who I am—and just answer my question."

"Why are you so interested?"

"I want details, Leon. Hundreds of details. So I can see if you're telling me the truth."

"I could give you thousands of details and they could all be invented by me."

"In the end, I'd know. When you've worked with kids as much as I have . . . If they don't want to give you details about something, it's because they're lying. So . . ."

"I just didn't want you to have a false impression of Claudia, that's why I— When you're in exile, you end up doing things you never thought you—talents that you had back home and that were just for entertainment, pastimes . . . Claudia is an amazing cook. Better than a professional, though that wasn't her—she was a lawyer, but when we arrived in Paris, our organization decided she should work in benefit dinners. That's how we met Antoinette Severet. I was serving her table—Antoinette was an enormously fat woman who had wiped her plate clean, mopping the sauce from her plate, and was already eyeing the gravy on the plate next to hers. Antoinette—"

"Hold it. That's her real name?"

"Yes."

"A miracle! You're giving me the real name of somebody involved in this—?"

"Yes. It doesn't matter anymore if you know her real name. Anyway—I can still remember how, just as I was leaning forward with her dessert, I felt this weighty hand pulling at my shoulder and a voice that was sweet and soft—you would never have expected it to come from that chest, believe me—that voice murmuring to me if I'd be so good as to introduce her to the cook so as to congratulate her. And when Claudia appeared, Antoinette said she had a proposition for her, but she could only explain herself when her father, who was on his deathbed at this very moment, had finished dying. Am I boring you?"

"Just go on."

"A month later she invited us to her father's funeral and as they were lowering his body into the earth she said—well, you wanted details, didn't you?—she said to the corpse, so quietly I could hardly hear her: Now, Papa, life's going to be a banquet every day of the year. And then she turned to Claudia and wondered if she would be willing to send three meals a day to her home, the only condition being that the ingredients be fresh and natural. Claudia hesitated—we were, after all, in a cemetery—and as Antoinette must have thought that Claudia doubted her financial solvency or something, she added: You can see that I've just come into some money. And Claudia still not answering, so Antoinette added a little something: each time she particularly liked a dish, she'd give us a bonus on the side. For the cause, she said."

"And that convinced your wife?"

"The salary—and that we'd be able to eat as well, even feed some other refugee. Claudia was skeptical about the bonus. The woman's a miser, she said. And the truth is that it wasn't easy to get our fat benefactor to admit she really liked a specific dish. By the second day, Antoinette was already complaining, she had a list of suggestions and questions about yesterday's menu. But I think it was a way of opening up a conversation with me, poor thing."

"So something happened to her?"

"Why would you say that?"

"You said poor thing."

"I don't think you want to know what happened to Antoinette."

"What if I decided what I want and don't want to know?"

"All right. They killed Antoinette. A bit over a week ago."

"They? Who killed her?"

"We don't know. They made it look like a burglary. But burglars are rarely that brutal with—I think it's the same people who are after Martin."

"Who's after Martin?"

"Two men. I think they're the same ones."

"What did they do to Antoinette?"

"That's something I am not going to tell you."

"Why not?"

"A woman whom I—let's say somebody special, she gave me some advice many years ago: Never describe a dead person. Death repeats itself through words, she told me. We have to deny a language to death."

"She seems to be a wise woman."

"I'm very lucky to have met her."

"And she's here in Paris?"

"Yes."

"And if I'm not mistaken—she's very important to you?"

"I owe her everything. She made me who I am."

"And what does your wife say about this—relationship of yours."

"Claudia doesn't know anything about her. Nobody knows."

"You're cheating on Claudia with her?"

"I've never cheated on Claudia."

"Claudia is—is she beautiful?"

"Claudia is extraordinary."

"So this other woman is—clandestine?"

"Not exactly."

"And this woman—her name is . . . ?"

"Susanna."

"Susanna?"

"Yes."

"And what does Susanna say about Antoinette's murder?"

"She hasn't said anything yet."

"And her death—Antoinette's, I mean—couldn't it—couldn't it have been due to other causes? What I mean is that maybe it has nothing to do with Martin."

"Maybe. But other factors also point to a connection. A couple of men had come to see her—and according to her description they look just like two men who had been watching the rue des Canettes apartment, trying to get information about Martin—and the others. I know where to find them. I followed them one day. I think they're the ones who came to ask Antoinette questions. She told me all about it."

"So she trusted you?"

"Yes. I'd almost say I was her only friend. As I ended up taking the meals to her every day. She was so alone. She used to say that she liked being alone, that she didn't want any company, but I knew it wasn't true. Her complaints about the food weren't because she was a miser and didn't want to pay us a bonus. It was her way of calling for help. A way somebody that timid, that isolated could connect."

"And you connected with her?"

"Yes. And she ended up being quite generous with the cause. And with me as well."

"With you?"

"Maybe I shouldn't tell you this, but it was her money that paid for this hotel, your ticket, the limo, everything."

"She knew it was for . . . ?"

"An emergency."

"And she just gave it to you, just like that?"

"You really want to know?"

"Why do you keep asking me that? If I didn't want to know, I wouldn't ask you."

"All right, all right. It so happens that people have always trusted me, everybody, that is, except for you, of course. Susanna once said—"

"Susanna, the woman you—"

"Yes. Susanna once said that I was like someone who massages the soul: people know that I couldn't hurt them. They tell me everything, their sorrows, their hopes, their secrets, and I'm like a human sponge, ridding them of their pain. Antoinette was no different."

"So you were her pimp."

"That's cruel. I didn't expect it from you, Barbara."

"Maybe you know me less than you think you do. I don't like to beat around the bush: you were taking money from that poor—"

"It wasn't for the money. I loved staying behind with her, it was like a refuge against the world, both of us swapping stories while she ate, majestically seated on the chair where her father had once sat. I won't deny that, inside, a different voice was reminding me that I could expect a big fat check, extra money for the cause, not because she had particularly liked Claudia's béarnaise sauce, but because—"

"Though, to get the money for my trip, you had to do something more than talk to her, right?"

"I'm surprised you're asking me this. But the answer is yes."

"You care so much to save Martin?"

"And you."

"I don't need anyone to save me."

"I hope you're right, Barbara."

I see her breathing deeply, then putting the receiver down. She opens her wallet, takes out some photos, looks at them, strokes them as if they were somebody's skin. She looks up suddenly, as if startled, catches a blurred glimpse of herself in the windowpane. She puts down the photographs and lifts the receiver to her ear.

"And did Martin ever meet Antoinette?"

"No. But I did tell him about her—he was curious, like you, as to how we survived in exile."

"So he also knew her real name?"

"I don't think so, though I can't be sure if I let it slip at some— Several times during the week he was visiting Paris, I maneuvered him toward our neighborhood and I left him at the corner café sipping a crème while I went to take Antoinette her meal. I didn't want Claudia to be burdened with all the work—that whole week, before I went out to meet Martin, I could hear Claudia muttering in our little kitchen—Marie Antoinette, she called her, she said she was going to cut that fat woman's throat if she kept on complaining."

"Claudia hated her?"

"Maybe hate is too strong a word. Claudia would always say that ten prisoners in Dachau could live a whole month with what that woman was spending on a canard à l'orange, and then Claudia would recite all the sadness, the whole list of this century's tragedies, all the while chopping the parsley and beating the eggs and boiling the broccoli."

"She was jealous."

"Who?"

"Your wife. She was jealous because you spent so much time with Antoinette, because you'd sit and tell her stories for hours on end. Right? Don't tell me you're not good at telling stories?"

"I like to tell stories, yes."

"Like the one you're telling me now?"

"You're the one who asked me for details."

"You're not giving me details. You're elaborating, spinning tales inside of tales. It's the old Scheherazade strategy."

"The Scheherazade strategy? From *The Thousand and One Nights*?"

"That one."

"And why would I . . . ?"

"Like Scheherazade, you're trying to entangle me with stories."

"And my reasons for doing this?"

"Just like her, you want to postpone something. Because, like her, you're afraid of something."

"I thought you were the one who was afraid."

"I am afraid. But your fear is another kind of fear. I think that you . . ."

"That I . . . ?"

"That you're afraid of me."

"I doubt you're going to cut my head off the way the Caliph wanted to cut off Scheherazade's. Or am I wrong?"

"We'll see."

"Can I ask you a favor? We're on such familiar terms now, I was wondering—could you—there's a certain harshness in your voice, in the tone of your voice, if you would do me the favor of making your voice a bit more gentle . . ."

"Let's make a deal. I'll let some gentleness creep into my voice and you—well, what I really need is information."

"Ask away. I promise to answer as best I can."

"No stories."

"No stories."

"All right. I'm interested in your relationship with Martin. I still don't quite understand the work you do with— You would receive Martin when he arrived, and then . . . ?"

"I'd dispatch him to another country for training and make sure that his folks thought this was an innocent trip, his family, friends—"

"His lover."

"Especially his lover, if he has one. I do this with all the men under my charge."

"And yet it seems that there are people who suspect that Martin is a member of . . ."

"A member of . . . ?"

"I don't like speaking about this on the phone. If you people are who you say you are, you didn't do your work very well. If there are men out looking for Martin in order to . . ."

"But that's not because I didn't do my job, Barbara. You know him so well, but you didn't even suspect that he might not be in Paris these past two months, did you?"

"To fool me is easier than fooling those—"

"Because I built him—in just one week—a whole fictitious existence here in Paris. So he was able to fill his letters with false references to real streets, nonexistent visits to restaurants that exist right around the corner. Not easy, I'll tell you, one week to make an expert of someone who's—"

"You don't know how I pity you, you and Martin traipsing all over Paris like pampered tourists."

"Not like tourists. Hard work. Running like crazy to collect enough material and experiences to last him a whole year. It's like one of those nights of love that we know is only this one time and has to last us the rest of our lives."

"Spare me the poetry, Leon. Martin sent me a lot of that."

"You didn't like what Martin wrote to you?"

"Lies."

"I don't think so. Take that letter where

Martin—I don't know if you remember how he describes his visit to the Louvre . . . ?"

"I remember."

"I thought you might. Venus de Milo: what that torso shows and promises, what it knows and cannot obtain, the missing arms, the missing legs, and the warm woman who was the model, dead now for thousands of years and yet ready as then to make love, ready to make love in spite of time's mutilations, her breasts ready in spite of the stone that—"

"That's enough!"

"Why? Don't you like the words?"

"Those are words Martin wrote to me. You had no right to read them—and certainly not to memorize them."

"So what's a lie in that letter? What matters is that the statue exists, that you exist with your body, that the words exist to connect the two women. The only thing not true in that letter is Martin's life."

She doesn't say a thing. She waits for him to continue.

"Look, Barbara—when he described the rue des Canettes to you, he would speak of the color of the bedcovers, the way in which the Parisian impressionist sun was refracted by the dirty windows, the sounds rising from the narrow street down there as if from a canyon, the smell of pizza from the faux-Italian canteens down below . . ."

"Yes, he did describe all that to—"

"It was all true, he experienced all that in an apartment that a French sympathizer lends us so our combatants can remember something real later on, when they're far away. In order to deceive somebody elegantly, as Susanna once told me, first surround yourself with a multitude of half-truths."

For a long while, she says nothing. From the street, the voice of a woman can be heard scolding a child in an unknown language, a language which is not French. Nor is it Barbara's language. The child begins to cry.

Finally, she speaks:

"So you know everything about Martin, huh?"

"An exaggeration to say everything. At first, only the surface of his identity, the facts that were in the dossier that Martin prepared before leaving—his parents, his vaccinations, his excursions to the mountains, his friends from school who hadn't joined the Youth. Later on, I slowly began to extract from him things that he had hidden, during the week we spent together, almost as if I were his confessor."

"Things about me."

"Yes."

"What things?"

"Everything."

"What things?"

"Everything. Your tastes, your favorite words, the protection your father gives you, your mother's death, the money she left you, how you've used it to help those kids, how you ask them to go out and photograph their dreams—everything."

"And what did he know about you?"

"Nothing."

"Not even your name."

"No."

"Security reasons, huh?"

"Yes."

"You like that, right? Getting to know everyone else's private life—"

"Private life is an illusion in our world, Barbara. When you can torture one person, private life ends for everybody else."

"But you do like to know everything about other people while they know nothing about you. Come on. Admit it."

"No. In fact, I don't like it one bit. If you knew the need I had to tell Martin something about myself, piece together for someone beautiful like him the fragments of my life."

"But you're telling me."

"Yes."

"Why me?"

"It's not the first time."

"I don't understand."

"It doesn't matter."

"Tell me."

"It's just that I—I corrected Martin's letters. And the letters of the others as well."

"Why?"

"In case Martin or any of the others committed some sort of error in their letters—I had to read them before sending them back home with French stamps—to make sure, for instance, that they hadn't made any mistake about the weather, you know, if it hadn't rained in Paris and they said it had, that sort of thing, so many ways they could betray that they weren't here. Then I'd correct what they wrote or I'd add a postscript or something. Just in case there was an emergency, we had a good supply of paper signed by Martin and the others, so we could— Let's say a relative had decided to pay a visit—not many cases of that, I'll admit, it's so hard leaving the country—but once an uncle of Franz's announced he was coming to visit. So I quickly sent him a note in Franz's name saying that Franz was traveling in Italy, so his absence wouldn't arouse suspicions."

"And that uncle, those people, didn't realize that there had been a substitution?"

"Context is ninety percent of verisimilitude. What I mean is that when our good uncle opened that letter from Paris, signed by Franz, full of details about life here, it never crossed his mind that it could have been written by someone else. Context—and, naturally, ingenuousness. People believe what they want to believe."

"Not always."

"You mean you realized?"

"What if I were to tell you that I did realize something."

"What?"

"Something."

"Are you sure?"

"Not really."

Now he is the one who does not answer.

The moment of silence grows. If someone were listening, he would not even hear the flies buzzing, as if everything that lives and moves in that room had been contaminated by the stillness. Not even her heartbeat would register. If someone were trying to record it.

He is the one who breaks that silence:

"It must be your imagination."

"Must be."

"And also, in your case, there's an additional reason. I'm—I'm going to tell you something nobody knows."

"You're going to tell me your real name."

"Not yet. I'm going to tell you something that happened to me a long time ago."

"How old were you?"

"I had just turned twelve. I had an older brother. Let's call him Pablo. He protected me—the older kids in our school wanted to hurt me."

"Hurt you?"

"Yes. They all wanted to beat me up. It must have been something in my face—the kind of face that people want to hurt. One day my brother couldn't care for me anymore—he had to leave school, and I found myself alone—or I would have really been alone if I hadn't discovered, thanks to Susanna's advice—"

"Her, again!"

"Yes, her again."

"You know her from that far back?"

"Since the night I turned twelve years old. Lucky for me. Because I discovered, thanks to her, that there was a way of buying protection against the school bullies. You must know people who are good at imitating voices. Well, I happen to be good at imitating other people's writing."

"So, besides violating private correspondence, now you're a forger?"

"I don't like that word, but I'll admit that in the beginning, yes, I'd say I was no more than an ordinary copycat. Teachers would send notes complaining about students' bad grades or misconduct and I would forge their parents' signature. But it didn't take long for me to outstrip that stage of mediocre plagiarism and go on to more creative efforts, as Susanna had suggested, composing a series of letters, ever more elaborate excuses, even suggestions. Thanks to me, an increasing number of my schoolmates were able to play hooky safely whenever they felt like it. My biggest victory came the day when the principal of the school showed my own father a rather insolent note that I had written on his behalf protesting some horrible sausages they had been forcing us to eat, and my dad recognized that he had written it, though he afterwards confessed to me that his memory must be playing tricks on him because he couldn't remember having sent anything of the kind. But what mattered is that he agreed with its contents: it mirrored his style and his thoughts. That's when I realized that Susanna was right: more than the mechanics of the handwriting itself, I was imitating people's deepest emotions when they sat down to write something. Their soul."

"You believe in the soul?"

"No."

Both of them laugh simultaneously. Then they grow quiet.

"And why did you need Susanna to discover that you had that special talent?"

"I had nobody else in the world. Nobody who cared, who knew me well enough to understand that what you call my special talent originated in that sponge-like quality of mine I just mentioned, that capacity for empathy with others, the ability to live them from within and, eventually, convince them of something that, deep down, they really want."

"Well, if you have that ability, maybe you can guess how I'm feeling right now."

"Feeling—about what?"

"About the fact that you've been spying on me without my consent, that you violated my privacy."

"I already told you that privacy in a world like ours is an illusion, Barbara. Or do you think that the men who govern our country respect privacy? If they get hold of Martin . . ."

"And because they spy, that gives you the right to spy?"

"Yes. In order to survive in the world they made, the world I inherited, yes, I'll do that and much more."

"Meaning that you had Martin in your hands."

"I don't understand."

"His destiny. His life, his death, depended on you."

"Just like the others. No more, no less than the others."

"And he had no other alternative: he had to trust you, entirely, right?"

"I don't like it when you speak to me that way."

"Answer me. Did he have an alternative?"

"No."

"Because without trust, or so it seems, it's impossible for you people to confront your enemies, right? In other words, Martin believed blindly in the one person his Organization had designated as his contact? Or am I wrong?"

"You're not wrong. Trust is essential in clandestine work. It's like the air we breathe."

"And if that trust is broken, nothing is left, then?"

"No. There's still faith in victory, faith in the cause."

"And if that faith disappears?"

"Then we're screwed."

"I'd say you're already screwed. God! All this is so immoral."

"What's immoral?"

"All this. Building everything on lies and manipulations. From the start you—wait, wait. You're the one who wrote that message I thought came from Martin asking me to—?"

"I wrote it, yes."

"So he doesn't even know I'm here."

"Ask him when he arrives."

"So he doesn't even know."

"I didn't say that."

The woman waits for another instant, again she breathes deeply, puts the receiver down next to the camera on the pillow, and looks at both black objects as if they were ominously identical, almost as if they were giant insects. She covers the camera with the sheets and picks up the phone again.

"And when did Martin first speak to you about me?"

"I knew about you from the dossier. We went to a café, the one at the corner of the Place Saint-Sulpice, since you're so interested in details, to make out a list of who might be writing to him, and your name leapt out immediately."

"What did he say about me?"

"Twenty years old, splendid, precocious, bronzed skin, unbridled energy, he told me how you recruited those boys and taught them how to take photographs of their dreams, that the result was incredible, that you were yourself a photographer with an eye for—"

"And did he seem in love?"

"Too much in love."

"And did he tell you we were going to marry as soon as he came back?"

"Yes."

"And also that we never lied to each other?"

"He never told me that."

"That was at the center of our relationship."

"So . . . ?"

"So I don't know if I'll be able to marry him anymore. Not after all this."

"You shouldn't judge him too harshly. If you knew how badly he felt at having to deceive you. My heart breaks when I have to lie to her. That's what he said. And I answered that someday he'd tell you and you'd forgive him."

"You said that to all of them, didn't you? The same words? Because they all must have agreed to lie to the people they loved, just like he did, right?"

"I said the same thing to all of them. And I prayed that it would turn out to be true, though I supposed that many of them would never be forgiven."

"And were they?"

"Many weren't, when they got back, when the truth was revealed. Several times I heard that the relationship had been ruined by so many falsehoods. I would talk it over with Claudia and she would comfort me, because I was really anguished: she'd say, bless her, that a relationship which can't withstand that sort of test isn't worth saving. But that's not so: there are absolutely wonderful love affairs which can be destroyed by a lie, one lie."

"But that didn't stop you from repeating the same words to Martin."

"I said to him what I had told each one of them: you'll come out stronger, I said, you and your love, stronger because of this crossing of the desert, a

French phrase that I asked Martin to note for use in some future letter of his, which in fact I think he mentioned to you later on, *la traversée du desert*. He looked at me with such sadness in his eyes . . . But I'm boring you. You'll accuse me of being like Scheherazade."

"On the contrary, Mr. Scheherazade. You can take all the time you want . . ."

"We don't have a thousand and one nights."

". . . as long as you stick to talking about Martin."

" 'I'm scared that we'll part,' Martin told me, scraping the sticky sugar at the bottom of his cup with a small spoon, as if he were excavating something in his cup. 'What sort of future relationship,' Martin told me, 'can I develop with someone if I can't tell her what I'm doing, who I am, if she thinks that with these Fascists in power I've decided to go off and do postgraduate work in architecture in Paris, as if I didn't give a damn?' So I asked him: 'Does she really think you're a coward or—worse still—indifferent?' "

"And what did he answer?"

" 'What's dangerous,' he said, 'is that she doesn't think badly of me at all. She suspects I'm involved in something political, she even asked me, just like that, unexpectedly, before I left. 'You're going to France to do—something else.' "

"I never said those words."

"He says you did. 'That woman is like an X-ray machine,' he said to me. 'It's as if she could read your thoughts, it's amazing'—so he was convinced that you had guessed about his secret life."

"I would never talk about that sort of thing with him. With anybody."

"Well, Martin convinced me that you had. He told me he had had to make a real effort, or so he said, so you would think he was in fact a coward, but all the while hoping that you would know he was lying, that he was really a member of the resistance. 'Whatever happens, I'll lose her,' he said to me."

"He said that?"

"That's what he said. I'm going to lose her. I know I'm going to lose her."

"And then what happened?"

"Then he took out your photograph."

"My photograph?"

"Yes. And he handed it to me."

"And what did you think?"

"About what?"

"About me."

"What did I think when I saw your photograph?"

"Yes."

"Why are you asking?"

"That was the first time you saw me, right? What did you think of me?"

There is a long period of silence. If it were not for the slight, faraway breathing of that man, she could convince herself that there is nobody on the other end of the line. When he speaks, it is in a murmur so low that she can barely hear him, as if he were frightened of his own words.

"I don't know how to answer you, Barbara."

"I don't understand."

"I think you do. That you've understood ever since we started to speak on the phone."

"Understood what?"

"You said I was scared. That I wanted to postpone something."

"I think that's what I said."

"This is what I wanted to postpone. This moment."

"The moment when you have to talk to me about myself?"

"The moment when I have to talk to you about what I felt when I saw your photograph. I'm going to tell you and then I'm going to hang up. I'll call you later. An hour from now."

"What can you say that is so terrible?"

"You know."

"No. I don't."

"You know that Martin carefully opened his wallet and brought out the photograph and . . ."

"And . . . ?"

"And it was her."

"Her?"

"Her. Mathematically, exactly, definitely her."

"Who?"

"The woman of my dreams. A woman I've been dreaming with every night of my life since I was twelve. It was you, Susanna."

And then she hears the click he had promised.

I've never told anyone about her.

She said I shouldn't. Don't tell anyone, she said to me the night when she made her first appearance. They won't believe you. And when they ask your age, lie to them, tell them you exist, as they do, since the day you were born. Don't tell them the truth, she would insist each time she could, don't even think of telling them that your life only began the night you dreamt me. Don't tell anyone.

And I obeyed her, I obeyed her orders, the woman of my dreams.

The woman of my dreams!

Words that so easily come to her mouth and my mouth but that in the mouths of any other person seem empty, trivial, false, even an insult. The woman of my dreams, men say, so as to conquer an unwilling member of the female sex, the woman of my dreams so as to flatter one who has given in to their desires, the woman of my dreams so as to impress their buddies in the bar, in the army, at a sports match, in the office, as if they had ever dared truly to imagine alive the fantastic woman who blessed their sleeping bodies only last night.

I hear them and I feel sorry for them. The poor idiots don't know what it is to dream a perfect woman, an unknown woman, each night of their lives, they don't know what it means to wait without any real hope that the next morning she will miraculously appear to you when you descend into the street, they don't know what it is to organize their whole existence so as to be prepared for that one day when she will finally decide to approach you in the blind reality of daylight.

They don't know, but I do. I dared do it.

I dreamt her, my Susanna, the woman who first gave me life and then kept breathing life into me, I dreamt her for the first time the night I turned twelve, and though we did not make what is called love, it was like a wedding night for me and for her, as if we were getting married forever, and I did not have to ask her nor did she have to promise that we would see each other again, because both of us knew that the next night she would come to our appointment in my dreams, and we did not have to predict another encounter to ensure that the second night that same woman would be awaiting me underneath my sleeping eyelids, nor get ready for the third enchanted night when she returned yet one more time, there she was, identical, intact, the same as always, and by the fourth night I asked myself why wake up at all, why not simply stay in here with my love forever, but my Susanna answered that I had to go forth and bring her back life, bring her minutes and aromas and memories of the world, and that if between one night and the next one I interposed days when I accepted the sacrifice of being absolutely awake, she would answer in kind by someday fulfilling her promise to find a way in the future to materialize her body in my everyday world, she would find a way of joining me. And I believed her, I always believe everything she tells me, and I began to live without her and also for her, waiting for her in the nights to fill her with what had happened to me, sharing what the world was like, and absorbing her advice, night after night, without exception each night of my life for the rest of my life, she was always there, the woman of my dreams.

She had been waiting for me, she said that first night, since before my birth, waiting for the moment when I would be ready to receive her. And I understood that first night, with humility, that it was not strictly I who was dreaming her but rather she was the one who had made the decision to introduce herself into my solitary world inside: I was waiting for the moment when you would really need me, she said.

That moment was the day when they came for my father and my brother.

The only reason they didn't take me as well was that the man in charge of the operation saw the birthday cake with its twelve unlit candles on my father's desk and he cut himself a fat piece and tried it with his fingers and after chewing for a while he said, his mouth still full of it, he said to the man who had grabbed my arm: "Let that one go. It's his day." And after swallowing, licking his fingers: "I liked your cake, kid, so I'm going to give you one more present: I'll bring your dad back tomorrow morning."

He kept his promise. Next day, early, my father was brought back. Not my brother—he was taken off to fight the War. My father found me in the same place he had left me, sleeping under the desk. I hadn't tasted the cake. My little man, my father said to me—you've spent the whole night alone, you didn't move the whole night. My father never knew, nor anybody else—because I never told another person in the universe—that she had kept me company, the woman of my dreams, I didn't tell anyone that she had explained to me how to survive the hard years that were coming, I have never ever told anyone that that was the night when I was finally really born.

She forbade it and I obeyed her.

I have spent my life obeying her.

For the first time, you may have started to invent something, imagine something that no tape recorder would pick up. That voice, the voice of the man who wants to be called Leon, it is difficult to tell if the thoughts you just transcribed are really his or if they originate in your own longings, whether, now that he has confessed what he says is his secret to the woman called Barbara, you are not beginning to make up words for him, construe an inner life you know nothing about.

But you are sure of one thing: that other man, the one who watches, cannot hear what Leon thinks, does not understand him as you do.

It is not because he is powerless, that other man. On the contrary, it is frightening precisely how much power that man has, much more than yours, so much more influence over the fate of Leon and Barbara—even though you are the one who has supposedly given them birth, or at least a space to emerge into, while yours is the name people will hold accountable if things turn out badly for that couple.

It is not easy to be responsible for their fate and yet be unable to anticipate and stop whatever inevitably awaits them, what has been determined for them by other men in other rooms. Maybe that is why you reached out to the inner voice of the man who calls himself Leon—as a way to proclaim your faith in him or perhaps a way of establishing a zone in this story which that man who watches them from a distance cannot gain access to, a secret he will never know. One little thing that you control, that you hope you control, in this story. The one advantage you have over that other man.

He does not know that you exist.

"Susanna?"

"Don't call me Susanna."

"If you only knew how hard it is to call you Barbara, as if you were a stranger."

"I am a stranger."

"Not for me."

"Don't lie to me."

"You know I've never lied to you."

"Never? Three hours, we've known each other for three hours—if this morning's conversation could be called a form of—"

"You have to understand that I've known you for twenty-five years."

"In your dreams."

"Yes."

"So explain how you managed that miracle: to dream me before I was even born? Or have you forgotten that I'm twenty?"

"There's no rational explanation. That's just the

way it is. I don't understand myself. If I believed in the existence of God—"

"You don't believe in God."

"No. But this would be proof of His existence. Though I'd rather not lose time speculating. I'm just grateful that you kept your promise."

"What promise?"

"The promise you made the first night you came to see me . . ."

"The night you turned twelve."

"That night."

"And what promise did that woman make?"

"That if I were patient, someday we would find each other and then—well, you would find a way to—"

"You know, Leon, things between us could ease up if you abandoned this puerile story that you've been dreaming me for twenty-five years. Why don't you admit that Martin sat down in that café and began to talk blue wonders about the girl he'd left back home, and you began to warm up, and then things got hotter when you saw the photo. I mean, you didn't recognize anything in it, but you—you . . ."

"I . . . ?"

"Well, you're obviously obsessed with me. You fell for me, let's put it that way. And the more Martin gabbed away about her as the days went by, the more you desired me. I can imagine how Martin must have bragged about my attributes, as he made the round of the museums, passing the Venus de

Milo, the Gioconda, the fat, womanly bodies in Rubens and the slender, long-necked women of—of that painter Modigliani, and in each woman he probably found something to celebrate and remind him of his lady love. And when Martin, feeling like a real stud, says to you, she's the woman of my dreams, you really begin to dream of her, you can't get her out of your head, your skin, your sex, and that's when, without quite knowing how, you decided to . . ."

"What is it I decided to do?"

"You decided—I'm not sure whether it was the week Martin was in Paris or if it happened once he had gone and you realized you could alter the letters—anyway, you decided to bring me to France under false pretenses."

"And that's your interpretation of all this?"

"Yes."

"That this is no more than a temporary case of the hots?"

"I can't know if it's temporary, but it is a case of the hots, that seems pretty clear."

"How sad, Barbara, that you should prefer such a prosaic, limited interpretation, when I'm offering you something so much more interesting and alluring."

"Hold on, there. Did you forge that letter in which you asked me to come here?"

"Yes."

"And you're the one who arranged for the tickets, the chauffeur, the hotel?"

"Yes."

"With money you pimped from that poor obese dead woman."

"I would not describe our relationship in those terms—but I will admit that I did take money from her, yes, that is true."

"And Martin doesn't know I'm here. The truth."

"Everything I did, I did for him, for you and for him. To save you both. The first thing I thought when Martin showed me your photo was precisely that you were in danger, that it was incredibly bad luck that you were involved with a member of the resistance."

"A man you controlled. That's what you thought. I have ways to make her come and see me, I have them both under my thumb. That's what you thought."

"I thought nothing of the kind. Susanna—"

"Barbara!"

"Barbara. For twenty-five years I've been hoping that you'd appear, for twenty-five years I awake each morning wondering if today will be the day. And when you are finally there, just the way I had left you the night before and the night before that and all the uncertain nights before that one, she in my dreams and you in the photo magically the same—Susanna, it was the one thing I had never expected: that when you finally crossed over to meet me, not only would you not be completing my existence, but—what I never expected is that you would be totally, entirely forbidden to me. Worse still: that I would be the guardian of your future husband."

"Right! So you began to despair and—"

"I did not despair. But you wouldn't understand. In my dreams you did, but now, here, over the phone, you're someone else, unrecognizable."

"Maybe you should get used to the idea that women of flesh and blood are different from women you dream. Tell me why you didn't despair."

"You were—"

"She. She was. Not me."

"She was alive. She was real. I had always been afraid that she might not exist—that I could have lived my life out—how to say it—in vain. Living for a mere illusion. Because everything I did, I did everything for you, waiting for you."

"Everything? Even your political work?"

"So there would be a world that would deserve you, so the world would be clean, without suffering, when you joined me."

"You haven't been too successful."

"No, I haven't. The world's never been in worse shape. And as it grew worse and people became more vile and my friends ended up murdered or rotting in concentration camps and we were alive only because we were lucky enough to be able to escape into exile, the possibility that you might make an appearance seemed to get further and further away: I had dreamt a world of wonders to greet you, without men exploiting other men, without hatred. And yet there you were. So if I lost my bet that the world would be a better place, on the other hand I had won my personal bet, I had managed to turn my bad luck around, your presence was in defiance of the worst odds, the statistics that proclaimed that we had no chance whatsoever of finding each other. What I mean is that you could have been born in Singapore or in the Belgian Congo or in Abyssinia or in Chile or in Palestine or in some other strange place or maybe in Poland or before the War or in another century, or not have been born at all, who knows if you weren't visiting me from a thousand years in the future, from another galaxy, another universe. How in hell can I tell where dreams come from? Among the thousands of millions of women who have lived and will love in the future on this earth, all the women I could possibly have dreamt, imagine the joy it meant that I had stumbled on one who was really and truly breathing the air of my very planet and time and country and language. And that wasn't all: it was a woman I could find and someday . . ."

"Someday . . ."

"Someday love."

"Love. You admit it. You see. It's just like I said. From the moment you saw the photo, you looked for a way to—"

"No, no. I didn't look for anything. I didn't do a thing. It was up to you to find the way."

"What do you mean, up to me?"

"It was up to Susanna. Martin might have her photograph and her future in his hands, but he couldn't contact her the way I could. That's why I felt no despair, why I could pass him the photo back without my hand trembling. It would be enough to go to sleep that very night, close my eyes, and she'd have the solution as she'd had it every night of my life. She'd find the way to keep the rest of her promise."

"The rest of her promise?"

"Yes."

"And you told Martin nothing about this?"

"Not a word. Just that your picture was like a dream."

"A dream? You indulged in an ironic comment?"

"It's a way of surviving."

"And what did he answer?"

" 'Better than a dream,' he said. And added: 'She is the realest person I have ever met.' "

"And then what did you do?"

"Nothing. My typical routine: we walked the rest of the afternoon through the neighborhood, noting the names of the food you could buy in the small grocery store around the corner and where the shops and theaters and squares were situated, we bought a couple of newspapers, we passed by the Sorbonne annex where Martin was supposedly going to study, we planned the itinerary for the next few days using fifty postcards I passed him, places where we had to spend a few minutes so he could remember them later."

"And you were able to go on as if nothing had happened? You could go ahead and spend an ordinary day with the man you were deceiving so—"

"I wasn't deceiving him. I was protecting him. The work had to be done no matter what. Martin's life—and now your life, as well as the life of so many others—depended on my doing the job well."

"And you counted on that woman, Susanna, to get you out of that mess?"

"She had always given me marvelous advice. Ever since I was twelve."

"Give me an example."

"Why do you care?"

"As you say I'm her . . ."

"You're interested in finding out if you're like her."

"On the contrary. I want to make sure that I'm nothing like her. It's disturbing to have somebody attributing all sorts of things to you and—so tell me, what was the first advice she ever gave you? Was it the first night she came to see you?"

"No. The first night, all she said was not to ever tell anybody about her. But advice, what we could call real advice, only the second night."

"Tell me."

"There are things I'd rather not talk about."

"It had to do with sex?"

"You really don't understand, do you? I never made love to you."

"In twenty-five years of dreaming about me?"

"Never."

"So you didn't like my body."

"Susanna, I loved your body so much that—well,

that first night, I was about to—look, I really don't want to talk about this."

"I don't think, at this point, you have a choice."

"Later."

"Now. You were about to . . ."

"I had the intuition that if we made love, you would never return. I have to wait for this to be real, I told myself, I told you, we told each other, and you murmured to me as the night was ending that I shouldn't worry, that we had a date for tomorrow, in tomorrow's dream, that you would come back as many times as I needed you."

"Which meant . . . ?"

"You spoke, she spoke so clearly in my dreams: Until the day, my child, when you emerge from the door of your dreams and find me smiling in the sun."

"And she kept her promise?"

"The next night, as soon as I was asleep, I saw your face dawning under the night of my eyes."

"Look who's being poetic."

"You're the one who taught me."

"And what did she say to you?"

"She wanted to know the sort of day I'd been through. I lied to her. I told her I hadn't had any trouble at all."

"What sort of trouble did you have?"

"I wasn't going to tell her my frustrating, imbecile, pre-adolescent day. Frankly, I was more interested in—"

"Interested in—?"

"Going on with what we had been doing last night."

"And what was that?"

"You had let me explore you."

"Explore what?"

"Everything."

"Not only with your hands."

"No."

"What else?"

"My tongue. My teeth."

"And I take it that you liked it."

"Yes."

"And that woman wouldn't let you continue your—explorations that second night?"

"Not until I told her all about my day."

"So what sort of trouble did you run into that day?"

"Susanna, Susanna—you really haven't changed one little bit. Always so insistent—but not this time, it's not fair to tell you all over again what we've already lived. It's like . . . It's as if a wife you've had for twenty-five years is brought to you one day after an accident that has erased her memory and you've got to begin all over again—I thought I'd be able to, but I can't."

"So if the woman you loved had an accident, you'd leave her, huh?"

"I didn't say that."

"Well, if you can't deal with me, you shouldn't have enticed me to Paris. Wouldn't you say?"

"You don't understand."

"That's what men always say when women won't do what men want."

"It hurts me to hear you speak to me like that."

"Did you whine so much with her? Did you spend your time feeling sorry for yourself?"

"Never. Not a moment."

"So why are you going to start with me, if you say we're the same person? . . . You want me to understand?"

"Yes."

"Try explaining things to me, then."

"Is this the way you treat the twelve-year-old boys you work with?"

"My twelve-year-olds are much too mature to be treated this way."

"God, you're irritable. Is it because of the heat? You know, there's a fan in the closet. That's why I chose this hotel—only the most modern hotels have fans in every—"

"You don't know how thrilled I am that you had my body temperature in mind when selecting this hotel. Now—you were telling me about the first advice that woman . . . ?"

"Susanna told me that I was hiding something from her and—"

"Well, well, sounds familiar."

". . . and then she passed her hand through my hair as if she were my mother rather than my loved one."

"Your mother was alive in that . . . ?"

"She died when I was three."

"So that woman was a sort of substitute mother, huh?"

"Every woman is something of a mother to her man. But we would never tell a mother what we tell our lover. And she was clear about that: she asked me to never ever deny her my pain, that she had come for that, to rid me of that pain."

"And you agreed?"

"And I realized that your mouth was not only made for kissing, Susanna. That it was also there so we could speak. That your ears were not only there to be bitten. That they could also listen to my secrets. It was the first lesson I learned from her."

"This Susanna of yours—I'm beginning to like her. So what was your secret that day?"

"I already told you. My older brother had to leave school."

"And now can you tell me why?"

"They had arrested him, along with my father. The night of my birthday. Though the next day they brought my dad back—but not my brother."

"What happened to your brother?"

"They forced him to enlist in the army."

"Your family was against the War?"

"My father and brother, yes, they were both against it. I didn't have ideas of my own back then. You were the one who taught me to hate the War."

"And your brother?"

"He was killed in action two years later."

"I'm sorry to hear that. In my family, we also . . ."

"I know."

"It's terrible to lose a war."

"Almost as terrible as to win one."

For a while, they both remain silent. From the street, all of a sudden, a turmoil of voices can be heard, rising and shouting and milling around in the hot air, mixing with the sound of the pigeons and the far-off church bells and then the voice of a boy hawking a newspaper, a French voice, excited, filled with urgency.

"So. Twelve years old," she finally says. "And your father made you go to school that day, anyway?"

"My father said I didn't have to go if I didn't want to, but she—"

"Susanna?"

"Susanna had told me that first night what was going to happen, the following day I was going to have a lot of trouble, but that I had to go, that many cruel things were going to happen to me in life and that it's senseless to try to escape them. But when I talked with her that second night, I was—well, scared. The bullies at school—with their soldier-strutting mentality—had made my life impossible. They knew my folks were against the War and they beat me up, trying to get me to admit that my brother and my father were traitors to the Fatherland, cowards, had sold out to foreign interests. And what made it intolerable was that my two best friends had joined the enemy. That betrayal hurt much more than—"

"Maybe it was a useful experience. To prepare you for what our country had in reserve."

"It was terrible to think that someone could smile at you one day and the next day cut you off, hate you. I can remember one of my friends screaming at the top of his lungs, while the others beat me up: Hit the bastard, hit the fag good. Fag."

"That's what bothered you most? To be called a fag?"

"That's what hurt me most."

"Well, that's certainly something we can't decide: what others are going to call us. Only what we're going to call ourselves."

"Susanna—that's what you said then."

"You're making this up."

"No, it's almost word for word what you said to me then. How can you keep denying that you're the same—"

"What else did she say? You tell me first and I'll see if it's what I would have said."

"We were in an immense, misty room, almost as if we lived in a palace, and she began to open the windows, one after the other, letting in an orange, splendid sort of light, and as she made me breathe in that light, she said to me: 'The best moments in life are when we don't know what to do, because only then, my child, do we discover what our hidden strengths are.' Would you have said that to me?"

"A bit on the cheap-philosophy side, but I might have. Was it then that she suggested that you embark on your career as a forger?"

"That was the next day. And she was also the one who, a few months later, remarked that I might be ready for more sophisticated counterfeiting activities—letters and excuses and so forth—until finally, in the last years of the War, I found myself forging false medical certificates, even papers that proved that someone had been honorably discharged from the army and was therefore exempt from military service. I saved a couple of lives that way."

"And when the War ended?"

"I left school and enrolled in the university."

"Always following Susanna's advice?"

"That mocking tone really doesn't suit you. We used to talk everything over, yes, who else in the world could I talk things over with? And she was never wrong about me. It was always as if Susanna knew my talents better than I did."

"And what did you know about her?"

"Not a thing. I tried that second night to find out something, but she put her hand to my lips. Not then, not in the years that followed, did I ever manage to get a direct answer to any of my questions about her. Inferred lots of things, though: insinuations, colors she liked, shoes that press in too hard and make her nervous, things like that, quirks . . . But hard information . . . 'You'll know everything about me when your body and my body meet in the real world. Let me surprise you, my child.' "

"She always called you my child?"

"I was twelve and she was twenty, so . . ."

"So when Martin started to tell you, you must have been surprised by some things, I suppose?"

"Not at all. It all made sense,"

"Even my photography work?"

"It seemed almost miraculous that the woman I had first dreamt when I was twelve would be teaching kids that age to spawn pictures of their dreams. When Martin told me what you were doing, I took it to be conclusive evidence that you were preparing, in a subconscious way, for your meeting with me. Wouldn't you say?"

"No, I wouldn't. It seems a suspicious sort of coincidence."

"What does?"

"It seems far more plausible that when you found out I was interested in giving artistic training to twelve-year-old boys, you concocted this story that when you turned twelve . . ."

"I really don't know how I can convince you that—"

"How about if you tell me about this Susanna of yours."

"Look in the mirror."

"No, what I mean is—that woman in the photograph was the exact same woman you had dreamt of when you were twelve?"

"Exactly the same: the hair cut to the shoulders, the same color in the lips, the same curve to the hips, the mischievous glint in the eyes, the way the clothes clung to the body, everything was the same."

"And under her clothes?"

"That remains to be seen."

"I see you have a sense of humor."

"How else does one survive?"

"And during all these years that woman never changed in your dreams. She was always physically the same?"

"I grew, she didn't. It was one of the conditions she laid down if I wanted her to visit me."

"And you had that much control over the content of your dreams?"

"Hardly any control at all. I was asleep. She was the one who decided everything."

"And you obeyed her."

"I was lonelier than a well that's gone dry, a child of twelve who had found someone who existed exclusively to rid him of his troubles. Why wouldn't I be inclined to obey her every wish?"

"A dream woman entirely at your service, whose purpose is to care for you, prepare you for the moment when you'd encounter her in your everyday reality, yes, you're right, you'd have to be crazy to reject someone like that. Oh, Leon, men are so vulnerable."

"Just what Susanna used to say. Men are so vulnerable. But you're more vulnerable than most men, she added, because you're going to spend the rest of your life absorbing the pain of others. You need someone like me to get rid of—and these were her very words—the dark water of your soul. She understood that nobody around me really cared about my pain."

"How about your father?"

"My father was crushed by my mother's death, and afterwards it got worse when they took my brother and then we heard that he'd died in the—look, the worst thing that can happen to anybody happened to my father: he fell in love with his own pain."

"Why do you think that's the worse thing that . . . ?"

"Because you end up not having a place in your heart for anybody else's pain. Look at what he did to me: my first memory is my father talking to me, talking and talking, about things I didn't understand, about my mother, about how the utopia he had dreamt of in his youth was further and further away, about the cruelty of existence, talking to me, and I had this unique ability to unburden him, to relieve his sorrow by merely listening to him. That's my first memory."

"So it was your dad who started you on the path to being everybody's confidant?"

"That's what I used to think, but Susanna persuaded me that it's dangerous to blame your parents for what we end up being; all they do, she said, or, in this case, all he did, your father, was use something that was already in you, a tendency, a propensity, something you were born with. 'Why should that image of a father pouring sorrow into his son be the first you retain from childhood?' she asked. 'Look inside yourself, look at yourself at the moment when you came into the world,' she said.

'Go deeper inside, beyond that moment with your father, open your body to that moment and look inside, and what do you see?' And I looked at myself in the memory that she was breathing into me and what I saw was a crack in that newborn child, something like the gash of a woman's sex in the center of my being, an invisible wound which up until then no one had ever noticed and which therefore no one could ever have healed. 'That's where the pain from the world comes into you and will continue to flow in, my child. No, no, don't close it, don't ignore it now that I have showed it to you. I'm going to help you discover what that crack is good for.' "

"And what's it good for?"

"You really don't remember, do you? You're the one who opened my eyes, you're the one who told me, when I was twelve, that that pain connected me with the vast pain of the universe. Go out and look through the streets of your city and you'll see that the crack inside you is part of a more serious and wider and deeper crack. You'll see that those youngsters who torment you at school, she said, are part of a world that torments many others in ways that are infinitely more cruel. So you can see that I didn't have much chance at hiding what had happened from you—"

"My God! How many times must I tell you that it wasn't—"

"Now you deny it, but back then I couldn't hide a thing from you. Besides, those kids had hit me hard in the face, and those bruises from my daytime life began to replicate in my face that night, and you comforted me. I can still feel your lips on my face. And with each kiss you would give me a piece of advice: fight for what you believe in, and a kiss, but don't forget to take care of yourself, and another kiss, because pitiless times are coming, tyrannies that will use technology as technology has never been used before, and a new kiss, and there are moments in history when you have to defend your dignity and other moments when you have to dissemble and fool those who hold power, just make sure that you're not missing any parts when we finally meet, all right, especially a certain part of your body that I particularly like."

"And that part was . . . ?"

"You know what I'm talking about. Promise me, my little lion, promise me that you'll take care of yourself so that someday you can come into me and find life inside me. That's what you said to me. Are you listening, Barbara?"

"Yes."

"But you were thinking of something else."

"I was thinking how much you must need that woman. I was thinking that you'd do anything to possess that woman."

"Not anything."

"Anything."

"Can you hold on?"

She waits. The noises in the street have begun

again, again that agitated voice of a boy selling papers in French, perhaps a twelve-year-old boy, like one of the boys she has left behind in Berlin.

"Barbara?"

"Yes."

"I've got to leave you for a few minutes."

"What's happening?"

"Nothing. I've just got to do something."

"But you will be back?"

"You just accused me of being ready to do anything to keep you, right?"

And he hangs up and she remains there with the phone in one hand, the other caressing the camera and the sound which rises from the street and the September heat of this city which is so terribly alien to her.

Why has it taken you so long to find out where Leon and Barbara come from?

Why could you not be like that man who, from his shadows, has known from the start their origins, that man who has used that knowledge to make plans for them and gain yet another advantage over you—and now prepares to intervene with still more ease in their lives.

It is possible to lay the blame on Leon and Barbara for being so secretive, skirting their own past, their identity, perhaps because they feared someone like that man could be listening, ready to use that information against them. Or is it that they were overly careful not to mention the name of their own country because they were ashamed of it? Their caution, at any rate, has proven counterproductive: they ended up blocking your knowledge, obstructing the one person who wondered about their country of origin in order to help them.

After all, so many people from all continents have passed through Paris hoping to get rid of this or that dictator, so many people have conspired from the streets and attics and cafés of Paris, so many women have come to visit their exiled men in trouble in Paris, so many have never gone back, so many have gone back to be killed. And far too many have been watched from the shadows by men who knew where they came from, what they said.

Did you try on nationalities for Leon and Barbara like a mother trying clothes on her children?

And yet—aren't you avoiding the real reason why you—who should have been attentive—turned out to be so blind?

For a while, you managed to deceive yourself into thinking, perhaps even hoping, that Leon and Barbara were Latin Americans. You remembered that many young people passed through Paris in the seventies on their way to be trained in other countries. They were even given a poetic name, "salmones." Salmones: a way of differentiating them from those exiles who could not go back home, perhaps a way of reminding them of the clear, turbulent, cascading rivers of their homeland, so they wouldn't forget they were destined to return to their place of birth to hatch new life like salmon do. You told yourself that here was a story lived by people from a country such as your own, far away from Europe, far from where you now try to register this story, lost on the other side of the world, a country nobody seems to care much about anymore, with a past nobody seems to remember.

Is that it? Was it homesickness that made you try to bring Leon closer, make him familiar?

Yes, you acted like one of those lovers who look down into a valley and there is the loved one and you hail her, and as she approaches, you painstakingly refuse to notice the little traces that don't match, a shade off in the hair, a wayward sloping of the shoulders, hands that are slightly oversized, you adjust to each wavering detail with your eyes and your mind, you pretend the differences don't exist, you don't want them to exist, you want it to be her, you want this to be your story, you want it to be her alive in your arms, until finally she comes out of the eclipse of your senses and into focus and there the woman is, standing in front of you, a complete stranger you have never seen before. And then comes the real anguish: where is the country, where is the woman you love? Where is she? Did she ever exist as you remember her?

But that is another story.

This is the story of Leon. Perhaps the story of Barbara.

Not your story.

You are condemned to listen. Trying to understand what these Germans who might be Chileans or Poles or South Africans say to each other in a city where they were not born.

"Barbara. It's me. Why did you take so long to answer?"

"I was looking at the photos I brought with me. The photos my kids snapped."

"You care a lot about those kids?"

"They can see everything, Leon. They see everything that happens today in our city—you're also from Berlin, aren't you?"

"Yes."

"And they can also foresee what is going to happen."

"And what's going to happen, according to your kids?"

"The fear, the hatred my kids reveal in the eyes of adults, no words could . . . If you saw those photos, then you'd really be scared."

"I don't need to see those photos to be really scared. What I need is something that will give me hope. Is there any hope in those photos?"

"A bit. A pallid light of hope."

"If you say so . . ."

"It's as if—are you sad, Leon? When you interrupted to—when you left, did anything . . . ?"

"Nothing to worry about. Nothing that your kids haven't foreseen already."

"I don't understand."

"You'll understand. Unfortunately, all too soon you'll understand."

She waits for him to continue, but he doesn't say another word. So she asks him:

"There's something I'd like to . . . I'd like to ask you something. That night you met Martin—what advice did your Susanna give you that night you met Martin, when you—"

"Nothing."

"What do you mean, nothing?"

"That night, for the first time since I turned twelve, for the first time in twenty-five years, for the first time in my life, that night I didn't dream with Susanna."

"What did you dream?"

"Nothing."

"Maybe you dreamt of her and you didn't—"

"No."

"And what happened when you woke up?"

"I don't want to tell you."

"You'd tell her, wouldn't you?

"All right. I'll tell you. I made love with Claudia. It was ferocious, despairing. I couldn't—you know, nothing would—come out, I just kept on going and going and going—"

"What about Claudia?"

"She was asleep at first and she must have been surprised, this sort of—well, assault I guess I'd call it—well, it's not typical for us, making love in the morning or doing it without both agreeing, getting ready, so to speak. But she seemed to like the idea, gave me a sort of coquettish smile, and her eyes closed with pleasure; but soon enough I think she realized that I wasn't making love to her. And I couldn't—ejaculate. I just couldn't. All of a sudden I saw myself there on the bed as if I were watching from another part of the room, from a corner, watching what we were doing almost pornographically, without joy, just despair and sorrow, trying to find someone, something I could hold on to, trying to extract my semen from inside as if it were vomit, lost, lost as I was back when I hadn't turned twelve yet, in a world without you, lost, and I couldn't find a way out, until Claudia said you're hurting me and I didn't listen to her and then she shoved me off her body and left me panting and alone there in bed . . ."

"And then what did you do? Because it must've been time to meet up with Martin."

"I just stayed there watching my—well, you know."

"What do I know?"

"My erection. It wouldn't go away. That thing

seemed—unnecessary, you know, irrelevant. I felt like cutting it off."

"It."

"It."

"Why don't you call it by its name?"

"I'm shy."

"After twenty-five years? How did you call it in your dreams?"

"If you don't remember, I don't want to tell you."

"How did I call it, that woman, Susanna?"

"You tell me."

"No."

"You see. That's why I wanted to cut it off."

"But you didn't."

"No."

"Why not?"

"You tell me."

"You still thought you might be able to make love with me someday."

"Yes. Without a condom."

"You used a condom with Claudia?"

"I always used a condom with Claudia."

"How about other women?"

"There haven't been any other women."

"I don't believe you."

"Not one other woman."

"Not even before you met Claudia?"

"Not one."

"You've been faithful to Claudia."

"To both of you."

"How about Antoinette."

"That doesn't count. That was to get the money. And you weren't around in my dreams to tell me not to do it."

"And how did you explain to Claudia the fact that you always wanted to use a condom?"

"I told her the truth: that I didn't want children."

"Well, it's a relief to know that for once your decision wasn't based on something involving me."

"You're going to get tired of hearing this, but it does involve you. There's a fear I've—something I've never confessed to anybody."

"Not even Susanna?"

"Especially not Susanna."

"But you can tell me?"

"Yes, now that you've made your appearance. What I was afraid of was that Claudia would have a little girl and the little girl would have . . ."

"The little girl would have . . . ?"

"Your face."

"You were scared that Susanna would be incarnated in your own daughter?"

"Yes. It was my worst nightmare."

"So you have nightmares, as well as dreams."

"Oh yes. Though in times like these it's enough to go out into the street, right?"

"And in your dreams, did you use a condom?"

"I already told you that I did not make love in my dreams."

"So Claudia was the first woman you ever made love to."

"Yes. The day I turned twenty, the day I was as old as she was, twins so to speak, Susanna said to me: 'It's time, my child, that you slept with a woman. And you'd better choose her carefully, because with your silly fear of harming people I wouldn't be surprised if you ended up marrying her.' "

"And your Susanna wasn't jealous?"

"I wasn't going to get close to anybody unless she agreed, so why should she be . . . ?"

"It just seems a bit strange that a lover would push her man into bed with another woman."

"If she hadn't pushed me, I would never even have made an attempt at approaching anybody—and certainly not Claudia, who was sort of intimidating. Susanna had to convince me that—but I really don't see why this intrigues you so much."

"Well, you know so much about me, isn't it fair that I find out something about you? Tell me."

"And how can you be sure I won't be inventing it?"

"Just make it entertaining."

"All right, then, let me invent something. Let's see. This was my second year at the university. We were trying to breathe life into the student newspaper. *New Dawn*, it was called—and it had been, before we laid our hands on it, a sort of tedious, solemn weekly, with deep-throated calls to insurrection, hymns to the working class, invocations of the future. We proposed, with a group of fellow students, that *New Dawn* should be—well, there's your word: entertaining. A new language, full of colloquialisms, with satirical, pseudo-interviews with public figures, and cartoons and a gossip section and a section where students could irreverently send in contributions—a paper, I suggested, like a boulevard full of cafés and discussions that never ended until—well, a new dawn would come."

"And this, of course, was also the brainchild of Susanna."

"I consulted with her about everything, I already told you that."

"And what was your role in that weekly?"

"She suggested that I could start a service for students where they could write in about their personal problems. She did warn me that I had to keep my identity a secret, that I should write under a pseudonym."

"Why?"

"She was always trying to get me to keep the lowest profile possible. She thought I was in danger."

"What sort of danger could there have been back then?"

"She foretold a sad future. Democracy won't last, she said: the Weimar Republic is doomed."

"I find it difficult to believe that anybody in a dream could have said that."

"I only wish that someone had whispered it to every German every night as they slept."

"And what pseudonym did she choose for you?"

"Don Giovanni. We both had a good laugh over

that, because, rather than a Don Juan type, I was a virgin who hadn't even touched a woman's breast. Not even rubbed accidentally."

"So how were you going to give advice to others?"

"I was—well, this may not be to your liking—but I had become a sort of encyclopedia of human sexuality. Due to the things that—Susanna used to teach me."

"In theory."

"She would—demonstrate what she meant."

"Susanna had a lot of experience."

"I never asked her. I suppose she did, though her skills could have been developed, like mine, from hearsay. I mean, anyone who read one of my columns would assume that the author had tested all the beds and positions in the universe. My first column contradicted my habitually reserved character, my monogamous stance. Armed with an insolent and sassy style, I exaggerated my belief in sexual liberation as the way to universal happiness: everything's allowed, no limits to what you can experiment with, our only loyalty should be to our pleasure, let's smash the old-fashioned links between couples as a way of anticipating and provoking the need to smash the social chains that enslave us."

"That's a mouthful. And what did Susanna say when you showed her your apocalyptic writings?"

"She was happy with them, because that way nobody would be able to recognize in me the cynical Don Giovanni, I was so shy and withdrawn. But she was wrong, perhaps for the first time. Because Claudia, who was studying to be a lawyer, had read my opinions and found them frankly despicable, vulgar, and counterrevolutionary, and swore not to rest until she could personally insult Mr. Don Giovanni in his syphilitic face, as she called it. And she managed to do it—typical stubbornness in her, by the way, she never gives up: she discovered the secret identity of *New Dawn*'s sex expert. She cornered me one midday in a small restaurant in front of the university. It must still be there. I was about to start my lunch when I realized that someone was examining me. And there was Claudia: in front of me. Something implacable in her eyes made me set aside my spoon, far from the steaming plate of soup I had been about to taste. 'So this is the famous Don Giovanni, huh?' The first words I was ever to hear from Claudia—hostile words, said in the voice of an angel. Though she quickly belied her angelic quality, hurling at me, without even telling me her name, a delirious diatribe that she had been rehearsing ever since she had read my first column: she flung in my face my lack of responsibility, and then she machine-gunned me with what in the hell did these macho Don Giovannis think they were doing, and then she salted and peppered me with the wonderful world of the future that we would never build unless we stuck very closely to our moral principles and she began to complain that if women followed my advice—and all of a sudden Claudia stopped. Just like that. Halfway through a sentence. And she looked me over as if she were seeing me for the first time. And then she laughed. And it was not a pleasant laugh."

"What was wrong with it?"

"It made me afraid. Because she then stretched across the table—inadvertently showing me a glorious pair of small, sloping breasts—and she stuck her mouth up against my ear and I thought that she hated me so much that she was about to take a bite out of me, and even in my fear I can remember thinking how white and even her teeth were, like a dream woman herself. But she didn't bite me—not on that occasion, at least. I heard her voice, scorching and lustful: 'A fraud. You're a damn fraud. I can tell. You've never fucked a woman.' And she waited to measure what sort of effect her words had. And, as I didn't answer, she added: 'And you haven't fucked a man, either.' Never in my life had I so needed my Susanna to come through the restaurant door and rescue me."

"But she didn't come."

"You were three years old at the time—how could you have come?"

"Well, well, you're beginning to sound almost rational. Go on. What did Claudia do then?"

"She began to sample each dish I had in front of me with her finger, sticking it in the food and then sinking it deep into her mouth and then slowly licking the edges—the soup, a stew, bread, salad, a strudel, one by one, each dish—until she finally offered a verdict: 'This restaurant stinks. If you want to know what a good hot meal tastes like, Don Giovanni, come to my house. If you dare.' She wrote her name, address, and telephone number on the copy of *New Dawn* she was carrying and then she left, and as I watched her tightly muscled bottom swinging underneath her skirt I found myself lamenting her departure. I liked her. I would have liked her to have taken off a piece of clothing with each insult. 'Give that lady a good fucking,' Susanna said that night."

"Well, your Susanna is certainly not the delicate sort, is she?"

"She speaks her mind, if that's what you're getting at. 'First fuck her,' Susanna said, 'and if that works out all right, you might as well marry her.' I asked her why this one, who seemed so—difficult. 'You should marry someone you can't fool, who will love you for who you are and not for who you seem to be.' "

"And what did you think of that advice?"

"Listen, I was sure Claudia loathed me. But I couldn't convince Susanna. 'What matters,' she said, 'is that there's passion in this relationship. If she weren't hot for you, she wouldn't have invited you to dinner.' I argued that her invitation was an ironic allusion to Don Giovanni, who had been invited to dine in hell by the Commendatore, where Claudia was probably planning to send me with some poisonous sauce."

"But she cooked you a sexy meal?"

"That's what you said that night: she'll cook you

something brimming with aphrodisiacs, to rid you of all your inhibitions. And that was how the woman of my dreams and the woman who was to be my lifelong companion became unintended allies."

"Except that Claudia never knew anything about Susanna."

"Susanna admonished me sternly: 'One more thing, my little lion. If your future wife happens to get wind of my existence, I want you to know that our connection will be severed. I will never, ever come to see you again.' "

"Am I wrong to infer that you hit it off with Claudia?"

"It was marvelous."

"You liked making love with her?"

"Yes."

"What did you like most?"

"Going into her. The moment I went in."

"What did you feel?"

"I wanted to go deeper."

"And for her? What did you feel for her?"

"Happier for her than for me. Because I couldn't tell her the whole truth."

"And since then she's been a good friend?"

"The best."

"And she's never complained about exile, the problems you two have had to . . ."

"Never."

"And if you had trouble . . ."

"I would turn to her."

"You love her more than you love Susanna?"

"I don't think so."

"You don't *think* so?"

"Up until now, it wasn't a question that needed to be asked."

"And now?"

"Now I can't avoid it any longer."

"You have plans for us?"

"This isn't the right moment to speak about these things."

"I think it is. What did you think—that I would move in with you two?"

"I didn't think anything."

"Now. What about then?"

"Then?"

"When you had your first orgasm with Claudia, did you think of—?"

"I didn't make believe Claudia was Susanna, if that's what you're getting at. I didn't fantasize. But you were present, next to us, if that interests you. Even in the most intense moment I couldn't lose the sense of my own hard being, who I was, the sense that my love was borrowed from some other place, that everything was, meanwhile, waiting, waiting for somebody else."

"And that somebody else was me?"

"You have her face, her body, her age, her tastes, her temper."

"There is something, naturally, which you may have forgotten."

"It wouldn't surprise me."

"You may have forgotten that perhaps I had

something to say in this matter, that perhaps I have plans for the—"

But she does not go on, because at that moment somebody knocks at the door to room 242.

His voice is slightly alarmed:

"Is something the matter?"

She waits. Again, knocking can be heard on the door. She immediately says, in a low voice:

"Someone's knocking at the door."

"You shouldn't worry."

"And what if it's—there are men trying to find Martin, aren't there?"

"There are men who are looking for him, Barbara. They think his name is Hans, but . . ."

"The men who killed Antoinette."

"But they have no way of knowing about you."

"How can you be so sure?"

"The Nazis would never have let you out of the country, Barbara, if they weren't positive you're not involved in politics."

"And who's at the door, then?"

"It's your lunch."

"I didn't order lunch."

"I ordered lunch for you. You must be hungry."

She hesitates for one more instant.

"Go on, Barbara. It's your favorite food. You don't need to speak to the waiter or even sign anything. It's all taken care of. Go on."

Outside room 242, there is a waiter with a cart. The man's face is composed, unreadable, and he does not move when she opens the door. Behind him, down the hall, she catches a glimpse of this morning's maid, the one who was watching her, the shadow of the maid swiftly disappearing around the corner of the hall. The waiter speaks to her in French, with some brusqueness, and the woman lets him in. The waiter wheels in the lunch cart. He carefully sets the table and then serves: beef consommé, brochette d'agneau with wild rice, a colorful salad, apple tart, half a bottle of red wine, mineral water.

When the waiter leaves, she picks up the receiver.

"This is too much food for me, Leon."

"It'll be good for you."

"How about you?"

"I'm eating exactly what you're eating."

"So where are you?"

"Nearby. But that doesn't matter. Let's eat. And careful with the consommé—the French serve it very hot."

She blows into the large spoon and then puts it into her mouth.

"Is it good?"

"Delicious. How did you know I like all this? Don't answer, don't—"

"Yes. Why should I keep telling you that I've learned more about you from twenty-five years of dreaming you than from one slight week spent with Martin in Paris? I mean, you're not going to believe me."

"And if I were to tell you that I'm starting to believe you."

"You can't imagine how happy that would make me."

"And you can't imagine how much I need to know once and for all what's happened to Martin, why he's in danger . . ."

"After we've eaten."

"You'll come to see me."

"Not yet."

"But you will tell me about Martin?"

"Let's eat. It's so glorious not to have to talk all the time. Just feel the food flowing through your body like it's flowing through mine."

"And how's my body?"

"You know your body. Let's eat. In silence."

You have been so obsessed with the man who is spying on Leon and Barbara, the man who it seems has been following Leon through the streets of Paris for some time now, that you have not paid attention to other men, other voices. Leon knows of their existence. It is that knowledge of his which has finally alerted you to those other plans.

You always thought that the threat against Martin would come from that man in the shadows.

You did not expect suddenly to imagine and hear the voices of three other men who convened in a room in this same city of Paris eleven days before the events you have transcribed. You hear them through the glass darkly of who Leon is, of what he has surmised and himself heard about what those other men spoke. He could be wrong, he could be making this up.

But history unfortunately assures you that the words of those three men you are about to copy down have not been invented by you or by the man who calls himself Leon.

Yes. It is midday. It is August 20 of the year 1939. Exactly eleven days before a woman who has just arrived from Germany will pick up the phone in a hotel room and hear the voice of a man she does not know. Three men are meeting in another room in another part of Paris.

"Thanks for the visit," one of them says. His code name is Willy. This is the man who Leon has said is his best friend, the man who developed pneumonia and was unable to receive Martin the day he arrived in Paris. If any of them implied to Leon what happened at this meeting, it must have been Willy.

"Let's start," says a second man, who calls himself André. Leon does not know him personally but admires him for his legendary place in the struggle against Fascism, his three years in the International Brigades in Spain fighting for the Republic. André doesn't live in Paris and has come here only to discuss this case. "I don't have much time."

"The facts," says Wolf. The third man. The man who heads clandestine operations in Paris and is in charge of Leon and Willy. Wolf has mined coal at the age of ten, lost an arm in the 1919 insurrection at the age of sixteen, triumphantly led the trade unions to an eight-hour workday in 1927, escaped a Gestapo jail in 1935 with twenty other prisoners. Leon thinks the world of him. "A month ago," says Wolf, "a couple of men were detected

watching an apartment we use on rue des Canettes. There is no hard proof that they were Gestapo agents—they could have been from the French police—but, just in case, we decided to stop using that apartment. It turns out we were right to be cautious. Two days later we learned that Franz had been arrested on his return to Düsseldorf. And four days later they got Johannes, in Berlin. They'd both spent a night at rue des Canettes. We concluded that our organization had been infiltrated. As you know, the man I suspect uses the name Hans."

That is Martin they are talking about. Martin, known as Hans.

"Why Hans?" André asks.

"These events all occurred just after Hans passed through here on his way to Moscow. And last week one of Leon's contacts—a woman named Antoinette, who gives us money—was murdered. She had been threatened by a couple of men who answer to the same description as the two who had been watching rue des Canettes."

"And that's why," André asks, "you had Hans recalled from the Moscow training program?"

"Yes."

"Hans knew this Antoinette woman?"

"According to Leon," Wolf says, "Hans never met her. But Leon did admit, under questioning, that Hans was the only one of his men he left in a café near Antoinette's house while he went to trans-

act business with her. He's the only one who could have followed Leon, found out who she was."

Now Willy speaks out, Willy who, like Leon, used to be a journalist—except that he stayed on in Berlin for three years after Hitler took power, he stayed there publishing a clandestine newspaper.

"The truth," Willy says, "is that Wolf is accusing Hans because there are rumors that Hans has been criticizing the Soviet Union, that someone in Moscow heard him whispering at the training-center mess hall that this wasn't socialism, that this was state terrorism. Leon conveyed these rumors to us because it was his duty to do so, but insists that he believes them to be baseless."

"Then," Wolf asks, "why has Hans recommended that we pull our training program out of the Soviet Union?"

It is Willy who answers. "Because Hans foresees Stalin signing a pact with Hitler any day now, and if that happens, our program, even our people there, will be in danger."

"Absurd," Wolf says. "Stalin is Hitler's worst enemy."

The three men talk in that room and Leon tries to guess what they are saying, what they will decide. In other rooms, across Europe, other men talk. Hitler talks, Stalin talks, von Ribbentrop talks, Chamberlain talks. And Leon believes that if he can guess what they are saying, he will be able to control his fate, he will be able to control the fate of the woman he calls Susanna. If he knew that somebody else is also listening, that somebody else has other plans for him . . .

At that moment, André clears his throat. He asks: "And what if Stalin did sign a pact, I mean, what would you say then?"

"Then the Party would have to stand behind Stalin," Wolf says. "A pact would give him time to prepare. Let the English and the French bastards exhaust themselves fighting the son of a bitch. They're the ones who encouraged him, who let him rearm, plunder Czechoslovakia. Let them fuck themselves."

"We're the ones who are going to get fucked," Willy says.

"We're going to get fucked," Wolf says, "if we keep protecting traitors like Hans, if you keep defending him out of your friendship for Leon."

"Stop bickering," André says. He serves himself a full glass of water, then takes it to his lips for only a quick sip. "What matters is that Hans is arriving from Moscow in . . . ?"

"Twelve days," Wolf says.

"And you're proposing?"

Leon strains to decipher what is being said, what Wolf might have answered.

"I'm proposing to send Hans back to Germany. Right away. No contact for six months. Wait for the Gestapo to get in touch with him."

"And if Hans is clean?"

"We reactivate him."

"And if they arrest him?" Willy asks. The question that Leon would have asked if Leon had been present.

"That's a risk everyone going back has to face," Wolf says. "If he stays here in Paris, he's putting us all in danger. Especially Leon, even if Leon keeps stubbornly defending him."

"What do you think, André?" Willy asks. "What have the people higher up decided?"

And now, at this crucial moment, their voices begin to fade from your presence. You picture the three men silently looking at each other as if they had all the time in the world, their voices fading from you both, as the mirror in Leon's mind blurs and darkens and now no longer reflects their words.

It is useless to try to hear them without Leon to assist. If he refuses to listen anymore, refuses to imagine their decision, there is nothing you can do.

Nothing you can do, that is, but ask why.

Is it that he cannot bear the thought of a world where the soul mates he has chosen to live with and die for, these men who are the best and most fiercely loyal of their generation and who will die in the concentration camps of Europe, could send Martin to his death without a trial, without evidence, merely because he has dared to question their dogmas? Is it that Leon cannot conceive of a life where he has to continue struggling for that better world he dreamt with Susanna by the side of men he can no longer trust?

Is that why he has stopped listening?

Is that why, like so many other men from other countries you know all too well, like so many who believed and will again believe in other causes, is that why he refuses to listen to the words that might destroy his faith?

Or is he afraid of something else, closer by? Is he afraid of himself? Afraid of what he will feel at the moment when those men decide to get rid of Martin? Is that what he is blanking out from any faraway listener, refusing to show you because he is refusing to show it to himself?

And now, against your will, against your own need for loyalty, you can feel, in the silence that grows like a sickness, the hint of a question surfacing, a question that you have not allowed yourself to even faintly formulate yet, because once it is asked, another question will emerge from inside that one, and then another and another.

What if Leon has been awaiting their decision, not in dread, but with eager, joyful anticipation? Is it not what he needs, exactly what he needs, to have Martin eliminated? Wouldn't that leave Martin's woman at his mercy? Isn't that what he may have been planning all this time, manipulating those men in that room as if they were fingers on his hand?

And then, with horror, you realize that these are the thoughts that the man who is watching would allow to ooze from himself, coldly calculating what is best for him in a world without loyalty, that man in the shadows.

But you do not have the time to ask if he is the distant twin of Leon: the question inside a question spills out and you must look at it now—look at it as if it were a stain darkening the night:

How can you know?

How can you really know who Leon is?

As soon as the waiter clears the room, the phone rings. She lets it go on for a while and then lifts the receiver.

"Leon?"

"Yes."

"There's something I've been meaning to ask you. About those—letters."

"What letters?"

"The letters Martin sent me and you read. What did you add to those letters?"

"You tell me. What did I add?"

"Nothing in the first one, but . . ."

"Martin mailed it himself before he left, we went to buy stamps the very day he was leaving Paris."

"But the next one, in that one . . ."

"What did I add?"

"The part about my breasts seen from a distance."

"That is why the forests grow, first to hide you,

then to let you be seen, someday so you may hide and I may see you. Yes. Did you realize that I was the one who—?"

"The only thing I realized was that Martin had never said or written anything like that to me."

"And you liked it?"

For a moment, she is quiet. In the silence, again the sound of agitated voices can be heard rising from the street.

"How could you abuse the trust your own friend put in you? Martin considers himself your friend, doesn't he?"

"What should I have done?"

"Told him."

"Martin was my only contact with you. I would have lost—before, at least I had you every night, but when you stopped visiting me in my—"

"Leon! It wasn't me! I am not responsible for anything that phantom woman did or did not do. Do you understand?"

"If you had at least turned up one night, only one night, to advise me what to do, how to get out of this mess . . ."

"And that's why you started to write to me?"

"Martin's first letter for you arrived and it was intolerable. To know that you existed on the other side of that letter, in the city where I was born and brought up, and I could not see you or hear you or warn you or—with Hitler and his voice separating us forever—and those pieces of paper in my hand would be in your hands in a couple of days and you'd read those words of Martin's, so formal, so bland, not one of them passionately true—"

"Leon, that's not—"

". . . while I could make those words infinitely better because I really knew you. I had a bridge to you in my hands. What was I supposed to do: throw it into a mailbox without adding a word, lose that one chance to contact you? And I had an ominous intuition about the future: I could see this stupid ceremony of incommunication between us repeating itself over and over again during the time Martin was in Moscow, until the day when . . ."

"Until . . . ?"

". . . the day when he'd go back to Berlin and his bride and I could never again—I didn't care about the consequences. I had to send some sort of elusive signal of my existence to see if she recognized—"

"You had said that to her? In your dreams. About her breasts."

"To you. And you remembered."

"That's not true."

"You recognized the words."

"They resonated. As if—as if they fit me, like a tight dress, like a sweater that clings to your skin and that doesn't need a—why should I repeat it. I wrote that to you in my reply. A reply you probably didn't send to Martin."

"Oh, I sent him the letter. I merely cut out the part which was for me, the message you were sending specifically to me. The rest was for him. Of course I sent it to him."

"How come suddenly so honest?"

"So Martin wouldn't suspect. I mean, how would he have reacted if he had received your— Listen. I memorized your words: 'As for my breasts, Martin—I did not know that their shape caused you so much pleasure nor their absence such nostalgia—and I begin to sense that now that you are far from me I feel you nearer than when you were by my side, closer than my pillow. Lie down next to your Parisian pillow, my love, and breathe the air from my lungs waiting for you on the other side of the border, on the other side of your dreams, so you may also hide and I may also see you.' "

"And that wasn't enough for you? You had to go on inserting words when Martin—"

"If you hadn't answered me, Susanna, I promise you I would have stopped right then and there. I left the initiative to you. Like it's always been between us."

"You know how I feel?"

"You feel overjoyed that someone in the world finally understands you."

"An idiot, that's how I feel. All those weeks, writing to Martin when all the time I was really—"

"You didn't mean what you wrote?"

"I meant it for him, for him, not for you!"

"Something was wrong between you and Martin. Otherwise, you'd never have answered my message.

You wrote back to a lover who finally understood you, different from our enigmatic Martin, right, who had always been a mystery to you?"

"That's not true."

"It's what you wrote."

"Deceived by you."

" 'I am starting to believe that distance is a punishment that can also be a form of destiny. You see me with more clarity from Paris than you ever saw me in the sad fog of our sad city. And I am also starting to believe that we'll fix—our little problem, when we get together.' Our little problem. What little problem was that?"

"It's not what you think. Nothing to do with—sex. It's the way he didn't care for the photos, what I was doing with—"

"I didn't write those words. You wrote them. Answering me. You knew it couldn't be Martin writing them to you."

"I thought Paris had changed him, that—"

"Because it was a dream Martin, right? A Martin as you had always deeply desired him to be? Desperately interested in you, able to make you acknowledge your own smells, the smell that comes from your sex, the smell of your own pleasure. Someone who connected you to your own voice. The truth—I've always told you the truth. Now you. Now it's your turn."

She doesn't answer right away. She fixes her eyes on a small spoon left behind by the waiter. The spoon has a few melted grains of sugar and now a fly buzzes around it, swoops in, stops, flies off again. She watches the fly's movements in the quiet, hot Parisian afternoon. Then she says:

"That was the sort of Martin I really liked, yes."

"He aroused you?"

"Yes."

"You wanted to make love with him?"

"I always want to make love with Martin."

"But this was different. This was new. Right?"

She doesn't answer. He waits for her reply a while more and then asks:

"Is something the matter?"

"Shhh," she cautions him. "Be quiet."

"But what's—?"

"Shhh."

She hears footsteps coming along the corridor. But they are not stealthy footsteps that want to mask their presence, nor are they made by only one person: yes, there can be no doubt, three, perhaps four, people are moving straight toward room 242, and they step down hard, authoritatively, not worried about disturbing the guests. They stop in front of the door and she hears a man's gruff voice outside, answered immediately by a hysterical, babbling female voice in French, and then someone knocks at the door.

"Someone's knocking," she says into the phone.

"They can't be knocking. I left definite instructions that you were not to be bothered under any—"

"Well, they're knocking."

"Don't open the door."

"Is it someone dangerous?"

"This has got to be a mistake. Maybe the waiter is coming back to—"

"I don't think so. There's a group out there. Several men, a woman. French."

"Don't let them in."

"And if they try to break in?"

"They can't. I left very clear instructions that—"

"They're coming in at this very moment, Leon."

The door opens.

She speaks swiftly, in a low voice: "Three men, Leon. And that maid, the one who was watching me this morning. They're inside now, Leon. I think they—two of them are policemen."

"They're dressed like—?"

"One is, the other isn't—but he's also a policeman."

"How do you know?"

"Don't ask stupid questions."

"And the third man?"

"I don't think he's from the police. He seems—"

One of the policemen, the one not in uniform, interrupts her, saying something to her in French.

"They're talking to me, Leon. What do I do?"

"This has got to be a mistake. They can't just—"

"Leon! What do I do?"

"Ask if any of them speaks German."

She interrogates the four, first with a look, then asking: "Would any of you speak . . . ?" But she doesn't finish the sentence. There is not even a glint of recognition in those eyes watching her warily.

Without warning, the maid breaks the silence, frantic, ebullient, almost triumphant. The policeman who does not wear a uniform spits something out at the maid. The maid stops. Using the same peremptory tone of voice, the policeman says something else, gesticulating toward the phone.

"I think they want the phone."

"Don't give it to them."

For an instant, she allows a hint of humor to creep into her voice.

"Given the situation I find myself in, I wouldn't say that is exactly an option."

"Are you sure they're policemen?"

"Yes."

The policeman in uniform steps forward and tries to take the phone from her. She retreats, presses the phone closer, bumps against the bed, sits down, and as the policeman keeps advancing, she again pulls away, slipping backwards over the bedcover, her legs tucked under her body.

"What about the third man?"

She looks at him. He is a short man, balding, elegantly dressed, almost the caricature of what an administrator should look like.

"I think he's from the hotel."

"Give him the phone."

She looks at the short man and gestures to him. He understands and comes forward.

"Put the phone to his ear. Don't let it go! So you can speak to me afterwards."

She does as she is told. The administrator—if that is what he is—does not protest. He puts his ear and mouth to the phone with the calm of someone who has seen stranger things in his existence.

She understands nothing of what the man says to Leon and of course cannot hear, either, what Leon answers in French, but the tone of the conversation seems cordial and polite, and several times the man nods affirmatively. Just when her arm begins to tire, the man withdraws from the receiver and with a formal bow indicates that she should speak.

"What did he say?"

"We've got a—problem."

"What sort of problem."

"Nothing to worry about, it'll all be cleared up as soon as—it's so stupid that—just stupid accusations."

"What accusations?"

"It's that idiot of a maid, she's got it into her head that—look, this is too ridiculous. Let's not lose time. The assistant manager seems an amiable fellow. He merely wants you to answer a few questions."

"I don't see how I can answer them if nobody here speaks—"

"I told you not to worry. I already suggested to the assistant manager that I could come over and translate, as I'm the one who paid the hotel. I'm on my way."

"You're—how can I know you're really coming?"

"Susanna, Susanna. I've been waiting for this

meeting for twenty-five years. You think I'd fail you now? It'll take me two minutes."

"Two minutes?"

"Yes. I'm at the hotel across the street."

"All this time you've been . . . ?"

"I thought it would be better to be close just in case, and you can see I was right. Give these people your identity papers and go with them."

"And what are we going to say to them?"

"Don't worry. We'll invent something."

"Maybe, but they—they—"

"We can't go on talking. They'll be suspicious. The only thing that matters is that when you see me you embrace me as if you've known me for a long time."

"And how will I know who . . . ?"

"You'll recognize me."

"And how should I call you when I see you?"

There is a moment of silence. Then she continues:

"I don't know your real name. I need to know your real name."

"Max," he says.

And once again she hears the familiar click of that phone and once again she lifts her eyes and then for the first time she slowly begins to look at each one of the invaders of room 242, who also look at her and look at her and do not say a word.

I don't know where they'll be bringing her from. I wait for her here, halfway between the elevator and the stairway, to make sure that when she appears she will immediately see me, immediately know that I am here to protect her the way she has been protecting me these twenty-five years.

The doors of the elevator fling open and there is my Susanna, flanked by the two policemen, pale, dignified, looking out into the foyer, searching for me. I do not move. I feel her eyes passing over my face, continuing on their way without the slightest glimmer of recognition, stopping on other faces, returning to mine, continuing her search.

The assistant manager, with an almost reverential and old-fashioned bow, now invites her to leave the elevator, but she ignores him. She calmly keeps on exploring the foyer with those eyes I know so well, and which nevertheless seem to disregard me.

Then the assistant manager clears his throat, insists again with a still mannerly gesture in which certain signs of impatience are beginning to appear. It is as if she does not see him. She remains like that, in the middle of the elevator, unalterable, examining over and over again the many faces of the many men who fill the foyer, every face but my face.

Several seconds pass.

"It seems obvious," the uniformed policeman says in French, "that we are wasting our time being courteous." I see the thickness of his hand descend on Susanna's arm to drag her from the elevator.

Now I move.

This is not how I planned our first encounter, this is not the way I wanted her to see me for the first time, but I haven't got much of a choice. I advance toward them and "Let her go," I say to the policeman in my almost perfect French, hoping that no one will be able to detect in it the residues of a faraway Germanic accent.

"If she cooperates," the policeman replies.

"She'll cooperate," I say.

He hesitates for a moment, looks at his colleague, and then releases her.

This would be the moment for Susanna to come toward me, the moment to find refuge in my arms, the moment when I will at last touch for the first time the elusive sweet skin of her hand and greet her breath warming my neck and feel the tickle of her cascading hair, but she gives no sign of wanting to cross and defeat the distance which separates us. She remains in the place where the policeman left her, without uttering a word, exploring with curiosity the face I am proposing to her, and I would have liked to have offered her all the time in the world to form her own opinion, to delve into her memory for some vestige of this man who has dreamt her his entire life, but I realize that this delay is putting us in peril: the assistant manager is watching us with a dubious air, watching her as she probes my face and does not embrace me, so I turn to him and launch an offensive:

"What sort of dump is this?" I ask. "An establishment where guests are spied on and humiliated publicly without justification."

"If there has been a misunderstanding," the assistant manager answers, "I'm sure that it will presently be cleared up. If we could step into my office . . ."

We leave the foyer behind us, we turn down a corridor, still without my having touched her, still without exchanging one word, scrutinized by all those enemy eyes, the assistant manager, the two policemen, the maid, who keeps flitting around nervously at our backs. The assistant manager stops in front of a door, opens it, and again furnishes us with that old-fashioned bow of his, inviting us to enter before him. First she goes in, then it is my turn, and the two policemen follow us, and the maid is about to follow as well when the assistant manager intercepts her, entering decisively and closing the door behind him. He motions us toward a couch, but she prefers to sit in the most uncomfortable and lonely chair in the room and I go and stand by her side, still without having touched her, still without knowing if the temperature of her skin is the way I've imagined it, still without knowing what she thinks about me now that she has seen me.

"So . . ." says the policeman who isn't wearing a uniform. "Why don't you begin by explaining to us why you, sir, are here at all?"

"I am a friend of this young lady and of the young lady's fiancé."

"So you can answer for her."

"Certainly."

"And you've known her a long time?"

"A long, long time."

"And you are also German?"

"Yes."

"Aha!"

"But I've been living in Paris for the last six years. Since it became impossible to live in my own country."

"So how come you speak French this well?"

"I've been speaking since I was a kid. That's why I chose Paris when the Nazis—but I really don't see why this is relevant to— Look, we're in a hurry. If you would be so good as to disclose your evidence for this ridiculous accusation . . . ?"

"You're in a hurry, you say?"

"Yes."

"To do what?"

"I don't understand the question."

"I think you understand it."

Suddenly, it is her voice which interrupts the conversation. She asks me, in German: "What's happening? What is this man saying?"

"Nonsense," I answer. And I say to the policeman: "This, sir, is the young lady's first trip ever to France, so it is impossible for her to have been spying, nor would it be reasonable to even attribute that intention to her, given that she doesn't speak a word of your language—look, this is not the way to treat someone who has just arrived from Germany, fleeing from the very Nazis you are about to—"

She cuts into my words again: "What are you telling them?"

"You've been accused by that lunatic maid of being a spy, so I—"

"A spy? Me?"

"So I've been explaining that you just fled Germany and—"

"That's not true," she says. "Don't tell them that. If they inform our government that I—"

"You don't understand. Hitler invaded Poland this morning. The war has begun."

"My God," she says, and her paleness hurts me, and the difficulty she has breathing hurts me, and her hands going toward her face to hide her pain hurt me, her pain that is my pain for our poor people, our poor country, our savage, cruel, senseless century.

"What is she saying?" the policeman who is not in uniform asks.

"She says she's innocent, that she can't understand how you can treat her this way when we are all in this together."

"That remains to be seen," the policeman not in uniform says. "We find her conduct highly suspicious."

"What's so suspicious?" I ask.

"Nine hours on the phone. You find it normal that someone should speak nine hours on the phone?"

"She was talking to me."

"Nine hours?"

"We had things to talk about."

"What things?"

"Please! What do men speak to women about?"

"And you were in the hotel on the other side of the street?"

"Yes."

"Though you live here in Paris?"

"Yes."

"But instead of talking to her in her room, like any normal person would, you called her on the phone, and spoke for nine hours. That leads me to believe that you have something to hide, that you did not want anyone to see you together."

"Look, can I speak to you in confidence?"

"You can always speak to us in confidence."

"When a man and a woman take precautions so they won't be seen together—well, I'm sure you understand that—it turns out I'm a friend of this young lady's future husband, but I've always liked her—so I was giving myself time to . . . you know what I mean."

"You were trying to steal your friend's girl?"

"I wouldn't put it so crudely. I wanted her to get to know me better before I—well, you know, suggest something to her . . ."

"But you just told us that she has known you for a long, long time."

"I didn't say that. I said that I'd known her for a long, long time. That's why I can answer for her. That's what I said. Look—why would the Nazis send a spy who doesn't even know the language of a country to . . ."

"What about the camera?"

"What about it?"

"It's an advanced model. Ideal for espionage activities. You supply the words, she supplies the text."

"That's ridiculous. Why should I engage in espionage?"

"What sort of work do you do?"

"Study."

"At your age?"

"I used to be a journalist. Now I do research."

"And that brings in enough money to afford two rooms in luxury hotels?"

"I have independent means."

Without warning, she stands up. Her blue dress lashes ferociously against my knee and I feel the nearness of her body like an open wound next to my body, so close, the impossibility that it can get any closer.

"I want to speak to my embassy. Tell them I want to speak to my embassy."

"I can't tell them that."

"Why not?"

"First, because they must be closing the embassy at this very moment. And more important, because they'll think you're guilty. I'm trying to convince them that you're running away from—"

"And I'm telling you again that you can't tell them that. I have to go back to—"

"You won't be able to go back."

"What do you mean, I won't be able to—?"

"You will not be able to go back."

"I have ten boys waiting for—"

"You're useless to them if you're dead."

"You've known all along. You have—and now you spring this on me."

"I was going to tell you as soon as we—"

"Well, I am going back, whatever you say. You know that I left—my whole photo collection is—and now there's a war . . . If I don't . . ."

"What is she saying?" the policeman without a uniform asks.

"She's very nervous."

"If she's innocent," the other policeman says, "there's no reason for her to get nervous."

"Of course she's innocent," I say. "Look, the only sin this young lady has committed, besides her nationality, is having spoken personal matters over the phone on a special day, so special that an overly patriotic hotel maid became hysterical. Justifiably hysterical, it's true, but if there is no other evidence . . ."

"Unfortunately for both of you, there is other evidence."

It is the assistant manager who is speaking.

And he is speaking in German.

"Yes," he says to me in my native language, while the two policemen smile, "I happen to know your language. We're not as ignorant as you think, we frogs. You speak French, I speak German. So I'm in a position to confirm that you two have been making up a story that you can't agree on, and I can also confirm that she does not know your real name, and that she wants to contact her embassy, and also that you have said that the French police speak nonsense."

All of a sudden, I feel Susanna's hand in my hand. It's like the hand of a little girl who asks for help to go down the stairs. I press her hand. I wish I could close my eyes and overrun her fingers, place my lips in the palm of her hand and suck the slight sweat leaking from her pores, invade her mouth with my own thumb and feel the carnal wonder of her gums, I wish that my wet fingers could descend to those breasts that Martin has described but which I know so much better than he does, down, down to her clitoris, which I fell in love with that night when I turned twelve. I had seen drawings in a book my father had hidden in his library, I had read that the clitoris was a miracle of human evolution because no other animal possesses it, only women among all the species of the universe, but nothing had prepared me for what my fingers felt when she guided them in my dream toward the quiver of her barely opened legs and that small elastic feminine nerve started joyfully to harden under my hand in love, my mouth in love, but there was no penetration, not even when Susanna began to arch upwards with a smothered strangle of pleasure, wave after wave, something silent in her asking me to visit her and complete the secret of my face in the near-darkness inside, no, I did not journey into her, not that night, not in the nights that followed, because I have to wait for this to be real, I said to myself, I said to her, we said to each other, and she murmured that I should not worry, that tomorrow she would return, she would return as many times as I needed her, which was to say that she would return ever and forever, till the day you cross the door of your dreams and there I will be, my little love—and now here she is, finally here, but there is no time, there is no time, I don't understand why there is never enough time for people like us.

My mouth has been waiting twenty-five years for the moment when Susanna's body approaches and invites me into her life, and what this mouth of mine has to do now to save her is talk and talk and talk, what I need to do is find a way of answering the assistant manager, who regards us with a triumphant air, what my brain needs to do, instead of saturating its cells with infinite images of her, is figure a way out of this labyrinth.

"It is true, sir, that we have been arguing," I say in French so the policemen will understand, "but tell me if anything she said or I said proves that she is an agent or a spy or even hostile. Anything? One thing? One thing you've heard, you've seen?"

"I have seen and I have heard many things in my life, sir," the assistant manager says, also switching to French. "Especially in the trenches, fighting against your country, twenty years ago. And now we are again at war, sir. And those of us who cannot go back to the trenches, it is our duty to help win this war any way we can. With these two eyes, with these two ears. This war is going to be won the same way we won the other one. We're going to teach you a good lesson."

Incredibly, the two policemen applaud the assistant manager's brief speech.

"I hope you're right," I tell him, congratulating him in a different way. "I hope you teach those sons of bitches a real lesson. But this is not how you'll win the war, persecuting those who have sought refuge in your country against—"

The assistant manager speaks to her directly in German: "Do you consider yourself a refugee in this country, miss, or is it your intention to return to Germany?"

"It is my intention to return as soon as possible."

"She doesn't know what she's saying," I intervene. "Barbara, they'll kill you if you return."

"Why should they kill me? I haven't done anything wrong."

"You have to trust me when I say so."

"He does not speak for me," she says to the assistant manager. "Could you please do me the favor, sir, of immediately contacting my embassy so they can clear up this misunderstanding and arrange for my repatriation?"

"I wish to avoid all contact with enemy institutions." The assistant manager gestures in the direction of the policemen. "Take them away," he tells them. "Of course, if I can continue to provide assistance in this investigation as an interpreter . . ."

"The Fatherland is grateful to you," the policeman in uniform announces to him pompously, "but we have people who can translate. You have done your duty."

He takes a pair of handcuffs from his pocket and with a swiftness which indicates how often he has performed this maneuver he separates my hand from hers and traps it in one of the cuffs. He puts the other one on my Susanna.

"And let this be a lesson to you," the assistant manager says. "So others of your kind never again dare to use my hotel to conspire against the Republic."

"Seven months ago," I say to Susanna, disdainfully, "this same little bastard was probably praising the Munich talks and coexistence with Hitler. And now he can't wait for the fighting to begin."

Before the assistant manager can answer, the policemen push us toward the door. Susanna trips and instinctively lifts up her arm to seek support, violently pulling me with her. The handcuffs tear into my wrist.

But what invades me is not the sudden scream of pain. Unbelievably, I feel a surge of insane joy, entirely irrational, entirely unexpected. I know that this is the worst thing that could have happened to us. I know that my plans have been crushed. I know that we're screwed and probably Martin and Claudia and Willy and all the rest of us. I know that at this very moment millions of men on this planet are readying themselves for combat in a war where many of them will die, and their wives and their children and their grandchildren. I know that new concentration camps are being planned at this very moment. But it all seems unreal and distant next to the fact that my hand must follow her hand wherever that hand goes, that her body must finally follow my body. It's a miracle: someone has come from outside us and, like a drunken god, has used these steel rings to chain us together, to bind us as if we were being married. It is as if finally someone who is not me were dreaming us together.

I let my hand go down slowly and she also has to go down with hers, and we look at each other. And in her eyes there seems to be a realization that she is also trapped with me, twins in the infinite and almost eternal mirror of our bodies.

I think she recognizes me.

And I feel absurdly happy.

You are lost.

He is approaching, that man you fear, his shadow is approaching—and you do not know how to save Susanna.

If this were a movie—and the protagonists were Americans, fighting some dictatorship in the distant future, the scriptwriters would be sure to find some way out, some way to save Susanna—and Max as well.

But this is not a movie and you do not know what to do.

You are not even sure if you can trust the man who calls himself Max.

So you hesitate.

And while you hesitate Max and the woman he calls Susanna have been shut into a police van and the doors have been locked and the motor has started up and they are on their way. And they do not know about that man who is lying in wait, that other man who has plans, that man who knows how to save Susanna.

He can save her.

If Max is ready to pay the price.

There is no calm nor is there kindness in her voice, as soon as they are left alone in the back of the police van and can speak freely.

"Son of a bitch," she says.

"Yes," he agrees. "Making believe he didn't speak . . ."

"Not him! You."

"Me?"

"All your plans worked out perfectly, it's just what you wanted, right?"

"What plans?"

"First you read my correspondence, then you answer it using Martin's name, then you bring me to Paris with this absurd story about Martin—"

"It's true, it's true, everything I've—"

". . . and as if that weren't enough, when the police arrest me you lie to them, so I'll have to stay here in this damn city forever."

"I only told them—"

"I wouldn't put it past you to have organized this whole thing as a sham—the maid, that assistant manager, the policemen, all in it with you."

He speaks slowly, deliberately:

"Nothing is happening according to my plans."

"Look at your face. It's—radiant. You'll deny that you're overcome with happiness?"

"I'm with you, Susanna."

"I've told you not to call me that. I told you that if you called me that again—"

"Why didn't you cut me off, then, when I—?"

"And lose my only contact with Martin?"

"That was the only reason you kept talking to me?"

"Of course. To draw you out. To get information."

"No other reason?"

"No."

"Why are you lying to me?"

"Lying to you? Me? I'm lying to you? You dare to—you say I could have cut you off whenever I felt like it? Well—I feel like it. Right now. I'm hanging up."

She makes a gesture with her free hand as if she were putting down an invisible receiver.

"Susanna."

Nothing.

"Barbara."

She still doesn't answer him.

Outside, they can both hear the Parisian night,

voices shouting from the thresholds, crowds hoarsely excited by the war, the war, the war.

"Barbara, we don't have much time. Let's at least try to figure out how to save Martin. We have to agree on a story, so they'll let us go, so we can warn him—"

"Warn him about what? To watch out for false friends who deceive the men who trust them?"

"In order to save him!"

"I don't believe you."

"What in hell can I do to convince you that—"

"You could start by telling me the truth."

"I've never lied to you."

"I'm tiring of these romantic statements. I ask, you answer. All right?"

"Whatever you say."

"First. When is Martin arriving in Paris?"

"The day after tomorrow."

"He was supposed to have been gone a year. Only two months have passed since he—"

"His training was interrupted."

"Why?"

"He has dissented from certain positions that—things that happen in any organization. Things you wouldn't be interested in."

"Why don't you let me decide what I'll be interested in. When you see Martin—if you manage to see him, that is, because it doesn't seem that . . ."

"We'll be able to, you'll see that—"

"Shut up. What did you intend to tell him, what were we to warn him about?"

"His return to the country has been programmed."

"When?"

"Right away."

"So what's the problem?"

"Apparently the Gestapo know his real identity. They'll be waiting for him. Or will follow him for a few months and then arrest him."

"And he doesn't know this?"

"No. So I have to find him, tell him."

"Tell him that if he goes back he's in danger."

"Yes."

"I don't understand. Your party is sending him back even if they know he'll be killed?"

"It's very complicated—but in the last weeks, since Martin came through Paris, several men who were in my charge have been arrested back in Germany, and there are people in our organization who accuse him of being the traitor, that he infiltrated us and has been passing information on—they think that the best way to get rid of him is to send him back . . ."

"And those are the people who make the decisions?"

"They recommend what should be done. A high-ranking member of the Central Committee has been brought in to make a decision."

"And you weren't present? You couldn't defend Martin?"

"I think they may not trust me anymore."

"You think, or you're sure?"

"My love, I'm barely sure of my own existence. But as they've forbidden me all contact with Martin . . ."

"So how did you even know he's coming through?"

"A friend told me."

"Willy?"

"How did you know his name?"

"You told it to me. The man who was originally in charge of Martin."

"I don't remember having told you that name."

"So now you're going to start doubting me?"

"No."

"Good. Tell me something else: how did you intend to warn Martin about the danger if you can't even get near him?"

"Through you."

"How could I possibly—?"

"I was going to tell Wolf—he heads the organization in France—that you had turned up in Paris, that you'd left a message in the postal box saying you wanted to see Martin. Then they would have to get you together with him or the whole operation would be jeopardized. So I thought that when you established contact with him, you could—"

"And that's why you brought me, so I could—?"

"I already told you I wanted to save Martin, but I was even more interested in saving you."

"I don't see what sort of danger there could be for me if—"

"For you, for everybody near Martin. You can't

be that naïve. They arrest him and the least thing that will happen to his fiancée is a one-way ticket to a concentration camp."

"And if I warn Martin and he stays here and I go back, what can happen to me?"

"If you go back after having contacted him in Paris, they're going to be absolutely sure you're guilty."

"My father wouldn't let—"

"Your father won't move a finger to save you, if there's even a hint that you've been sharing your bed with a member of the resistance."

"So I'm screwed, no matter what happens."

"I'd say you're saved."

"Irresponsible assholes. Deciding everything about me, without consulting me, you and Martin and that Wolf and who knows who else, you're just like the Nazis. You've fought them for so long you've ended up being just like them."

"That's not true!"

"What sort of new humanity are you going to build using these methods . . ."

"I had to take some action—and if I made a mistake it was only because you weren't present. In my dreams, we decided everything together. And now that we're—"

"Together? You call this being together? We're under arrest, handcuffed, cut off from the world. Who cares if we're—"

"At least, you'll be able to give me advice."

"Advice? You want advice? Stop lying to me."

"I—"

"I'll withdraw that advice. You know—I couldn't care less if you're telling the truth or if this is all just a gigantic tall tale and you're betraying your own people to get rid of Martin, the only thing I can—"

"Susanna!"

". . . the only thing I can be sure of in this whole mess is that you got exactly what you wanted: you forged and you maneuvered and you betrayed until you managed to make me abandon my kids back home in Berlin and come to Paris and stay here with you. That's what you decided to do as soon as you saw my photo, wasn't it? Those were your plans, weren't they? So I'd have to stay with you?"

"No."

"Don't lie. Now you'll tell me you aren't dying to make love with me."

"I'm dying to make love with you."

"So . . ."

"But only for one night."

"What?"

"One night."

"And all this for—that would be enough for you? One night?"

"It was the most I could hope for."

"And after that night?"

"That depended on both of us. If you felt for me what I—"

"You were going to leave Claudia?"

"I couldn't conceive of life without Claudia."

"But you haven't told her about us."

"I was going to tell her as soon as—"

"As soon as we'd spent a night together."

"Yes."

"And how was she going to react?"

"She wouldn't stop loving me."

"You're so special?"

"No."

"Yes, you think you are. You think that I'm going to fall in love with you, that I'd leave Martin once—"

"I told you that I'm not much of a lover, Barbara. I don't think I can compete with Martin in bed."

"What do you know about how Martin is in bed?"

"What he's told me."

"What men tell each other. So many things they tell each other. It seemed strange that Martin would write to me that the only thing he wanted was one night more with me on this earth, that the only thing he was asking of life was—"

"Yes, one night so we could do what we were never able to do before, yes—you knew it was me writing to you, didn't you?"

"And if I didn't cooperate once I arrived in Paris?"

"I never even thought you could refuse, not for a moment. If you didn't have it in you, if you weren't generous enough, to offer one night to the man who had been faithful to you his whole life, then that man would have to recognize he'd made a mistake, you might have her body, but you didn't have her soul, and so he'd have to erase you from his life, forget you. And keep searching. For the real Susanna. Because I know that my Susanna would say yes. She's that kind of woman."

"But I'm not Susanna."

"That's something we don't know yet, do we?"

"And how do you propose to know it?"

"If we make love, then I'll know, Susanna."

"Susanna, Susanna, Susanna. I'm sick of your damned Susanna, Max. That is your real name, isn't it?"

"Yes."

"Well, you stay here with your Susanna. I'm going back to Germany. I've got a life there, a language, ten kids who depend on me, wonderful kids, who don't have dreams of pornographic, impossible women, who dream of a different, healthy country—"

"A shithole of a country."

"Yes, but it's my country. And it needs me. And if everybody who hates what's happening leaves, than what's—"

"If you go back, they'll—"

"They won't do a thing to me. Not a fucking thing. I'm getting our embassy to send me back. They'll ask my father what—"

"They'll ask you about Martin."

"And I'll tell them everything I know about Martin. That is—nothing. Nothing, not a thing. That's why you noble fellows kept me in the dark, right, so I could never tell anybody about his activities? Lucky for me, he never trusted me with his—"

"I already told you that he didn't tell you because we decided it would be best for you."

"How long am I going to stand for you guys deciding what's good and what's bad for me and what's better and what's—I never asked Martin and I sure as hell didn't ask you to protect me. None of you."

"You want Martin to be—?"

"I want to be left alone."

"I can't believe you're saying this to me."

"Not like Susanna, huh? Who was a good little soldier? Who obeyed your every whim? Who did whatever the fuck you wanted, the woman of your dreams? Who would have sacrificed her life for yours, who would have lived her whole life among strangers, wandering without hope, Susanna who would have forgotten her own dreams for her man, for the man who was dreaming her. Well, not me. So start getting used to the idea that I'm not her. Because I'm not. Are you convinced now? Are you convinced that I'm not her?"

And exactly at that moment they arrive at police headquarters and the door to the van opens and the policeman not in uniform tells them in French to get down and before they move he lifts his chained hand toward a lock of hair which partly hides her brow and says to her with a sweetness that cannot be feigned:

"Not yet."

The question can no longer be avoided.

Has Max been conning you?

Has Max been fooling you all this time just as he has been fooling the woman he calls Susanna? Making you believe he's innocent, when all along he's been the one who betrayed his own men back home in order to blame Martin, in order to keep the girl?

If he did not betray those men, then who could it be?

Toy with the idea that it is Wolf or Willy or one of those others—but, then, what would their motive be? Why denigrate them without the slightest shred of evidence?

There is always, of course, that other man, the one you have feared ever since you and supposedly he began to eavesdrop on that phone conversation.

And yet, even as you keep announcing his appearance soon, you have started to ask yourself if you have not made him up in order to save Max, this Max you have bonded with. The need to ensure that this is not the story of a traitor is overwhelming, the need to believe that it is possible to tell in our times the story of a man who, with all his faults, was—yes, let that word be written here—good.

You strain to watch Max at the moment when the handcuffs are stripped from his hands, when he is separated from the woman of his dreams, when he is blindfolded and taken into a room to await interrogation.

If I could see his reaction, you think to yourself. If I could read his face. If I could be sure what he is thinking.

But then you lose him.

You find yourself again, many decades later, in this room where you write, in a country that is not your own, you find yourself here, a survivor just like him, without a plan for Max or for Susanna or for anybody in that world or for anybody else in the world who is in trouble, so desperate to establish your friend's innocence that you discover yourself absurdly wondering if perhaps Claudia could not be the one who has betrayed them all. You have not even met her and here you are, accusing her, with nothing to bolster your theory except the stereotype of the insanely jealous wife who went crazy because her man loves another woman and wove a rabid conspiracy in order to seek revenge. Surely your imagination can come up with something less trite, less conventional?

If this were a movie, this story would have a

happy ending, a final twist in which the innocent are rewarded and the villains are punished. Max wants to save Susanna? At any price to himself? Make Susanna work for the anti-Nazi resistance, helping them flush out the traitor in their midst—not the passive, manipulated woman we have seen up to now, but in full control. Make her deceive Max while he thinks he is deceiving her, do to him what he has done to her. Make Martin, and the French police, and the hotel employees, all part of her master plan, a way of ridding themselves of this agent who has been betraying his cause and the men under his command.

Who can be sure that this is not the way it happened, that this is not the way millions of spectators all over the world will behold Max's story? Do you have the power to avoid that sort of ending?

While you mull all this over and feel sorry for yourself and conjure up literary strategies and moralize about the suffering of the world, the only truth that really matters is that nobody is with Max.

You have left him alone.

There is, in effect, no way of escaping history.

One of those two voices says:

"Okay, Max. There's only one thing we really want to know."

"Yeah," says the other voice. "Just one thing."

"Did you fuck her, Max?"

"I don't know who you're talking about."

"Your mother, who do you think we're—the girl, we were wondering if you'd fucked little Barbara."

"No."

"So why'd you pay for that fancy hotel? Why'd you pay for her ticket?"

"I already told your colleagues everything. I brought her from Berlin to save her. She was going to be killed."

"And how come you're so interested in her?"

"I know her future husband, Martin."

"Who, of course, can confirm your story . . ."

"If I knew where to find him, I'm sure he'd—

All I know about him is that he studies architecture, here at the Sorbonne. I run into him once in a while at a bar I go to near Montparnasse—lots of Germans meet there."

"And he's also a refugee?"

"No. He's going back."

"So why would he go for a drink at that sort of place? Isn't it dangerous for him to . . . ?"

"That's a question you'll have to ask him."

"And when did you see him last?"

"A couple of weeks ago. He said something about heading for Italy to look at some monuments, some churches, something of the sort."

"Very convenient."

"Nobody goes around asking where anybody else lives—not in times like these . . . I don't even know his last name."

"But you know a lot, on the other hand, about his little fiancée, right? And don't get us wrong: we're not criticizing your taste in women."

"On the contrary, Max. If she were really in danger, we can see why it would be worth your while to try and save her."

"I'm telling you she really is in danger. I got the information a few weeks ago through a friend who had just come from Germany."

"A Communist friend?"

"No."

"A Communist just like you."

"I'm not a Communist."

"There are people who say you are."

"That's a lie."

"Are you accusing us of being liars?"

"Not you. Your informers."

"You don't trust us, do you, Max?"

"I'm the one who's blindfolded."

"You don't like to be blindfolded?"

"It doesn't exactly inspire—trust."

"You don't think we're your friends?"

"You should be. As we're fighting the same enemy."

"Wrong."

"As my colleague says, dead wrong. Because you Communists, now you're buddies with Hitler, aren't you?"

"I told you I was not a Communist. But I don't think it's fair to say that Communists are Hitler's friends. From what I've seen and read, they're his worst enemies."

"You read a lot, don't you, Max?"

"I try."

"Did you read the newspapers on August 24?"

"I read the newspapers every day."

"Did you read the news about Stalin and his toast to von Ribbentrop the previous night?"

"Did you read what Comrade Stalin said in his toast?"

"Did you read that he toasted Hitler's health?"

"And what else, Max? What else did he say?"

"He said—he said Hitler was beloved by his people."

"Though the next day you couldn't read anymore, could you?"

"I don't understand the question."

"What my colleague is referring to is that on August 25 *L'Humanité* was confiscated. You're familiar with *L'Humanité*, the organ of the Communist Party?"

"Yes."

"Or do you think it's right that Hitler's friends should be able to keep publishing their bolshevik propaganda? Do you think that a war can be won with a fifth column inside, people who one day hate Hitler and the next try to drink with him?"

"You must be referring to the people who a few months ago were trying to pacify Hitler, and signed the treaty at Munich, the people who let him invade Czechoslovakia."

"Well, it looks as if Max is turning a bit critical."

"It looks as if Max is shitting on the country that offered him sanctuary."

"It looks as if it might do Max some good to read another sort of newspaper, like *Je suis partout* from L'Action Française we've got here."

"I don't read Fascist papers."

"They may be Fascist, but they love their country. *Française.* Their name says it all."

"And at least they don't think this is an imperialist war, like the Communists say."

"Like the Jews are saying."

"Hey, Max, are you a Jew?"

"No."

"Are you sure? Not even a drop of blood? I mean, Max is a rather Jewish name."

"I'm not Jewish, but I don't see what that—"

"It's just that you began to make these gratuitous accusations—"

"Just like the Jews do all the time—"

"Right! And we don't like that, we could almost say that those kinds of accusations hurt us. Or do I need to remind you that here the one being accused of spying happens to be you."

"I don't need to be reminded of that, thank you."

"So we're not the ones who should be doing the explaining. We're not the ones who brought this little German girl, with her advanced camera, into our country. And we're not the ones who spent nine hours on the phone briefing her for her mission."

"I already said that I did it to save her. I learned from a friend who had just arrived from Germany that Barbara was in danger, that the Gestapo were going to come for her in a few days. So I brought her here."

"And that friend, undoubtedly he's here in Paris to confirm your story."

"I know this must seem suspicious to you, but it so happens that he went back—and the Nazis got him when he—"

"It's good to know that even you understand that we have trouble believing your story, Max, but let's suppose that what you're saying is true—"

"Just supposing, Max."

"Even in that case, what's hard to understand is why you'd go to so much trouble to save this girl and not so many others who . . ."

"I had personal reasons of an . . . intimate nature."

"And you don't trust us."

"It's just that I've never told anyone about it."

There is a pause. Then:

"Not even your wife?"

"Especially not my wife."

"Pretty woman, your wife, Max. Claudia's the name, huh?"

"And she must be prettier in the flesh than in this photo."

All of a sudden, a third voice can be heard, a voice that has not been heard until now.

"Pass me the photo."

"You can see that our Max here must have something going for him, Chief, because this one's also a sweet catch, a bit older than the other one, but . . ."

"I don't blame our Max for not wanting to tell his wife what he's been doing with little Barbara. Right, Chief?"

There are a few moments of silence. They expect their boss's answer. It does not come. Then one of those two voices says:

"But you're going to tell us, aren't you, Max?"

"If you insist."

"Maybe you could begin by explaining something: that girl says she's never met you before today. You, on the other hand, have declared to a policeman that you've known her for—let's see—for a long, long time. Your words."

"It's merely that she doesn't know me, but I do know her . . . One day my friend Martin showed me a photo of his girlfriend. Just like right now I showed you my wife's. But in my case—well, I recognized her immediately."

"You'd known her from before?"

"What I'm telling you has to remain a secret."

"Weren't you the one who said we had the same enemy? Or were you bullshitting us, Max?"

"You have to promise me that she won't know what I'm about to— Please. I knew Barbara in Berlin. Before I left. In front of the newspaper where I worked, there was a girls' school. Ask Barbara if it's so, if it isn't true that there used to be a newspaper exactly in front of— Every day I would watch the girls going in and out of school. And there was one in particular who caught my attention, she was so full of life, so savagely beautiful, with her hair flowing behind her when she ran down the street in the afternoon. It's like I'm seeing her right now."

"What year are we speaking about?"

"More than ten years have passed. It must have been '28, maybe '29."

"And that girl was Barbara?"

"Yes."

"And how old would she have been?"

"Nine, maybe ten."

"You're a fucking pervert, Max."

"Jewish, Communist, and to top it all—a pervert."

"I shouldn't have started telling you. I knew you wouldn't understand. It was an absolutely pure love, absolutely from afar. I never went near her, never contacted her, never touched her, never spoke to her, never sought her out, not even her address. Nothing."

"Don't play the innocent with us, Max. You had to have some sort of fantasy involving her, didn't you?"

"Everything else around me was crumbling, except her. What I least wanted to do was stain that little girl—I loved seeing her play, jump, above all I loved to hear her laugh. Her laughter crossed the street, above the Berlin traffic, above the pedestrians, above the first columns of marching, crazy Nazis, and it reached me at my desk from where I watched her. It made me young again, it helped me pass each night merely to think that the next morning I'd see her, it helped me pass the day to think that in the afternoon I'd be able to share an instant with her."

"Our Max doesn't want to admit that he was hot for her. These Germans . . ."

"Sex had nothing to do with it. You'd have to understand what it is to live in a country where everything is going wrong. The crisis—everything gray, Hitler's opponents bickering among themselves; and in the middle of that depressing panorama, there she was, straight as an arrow, innocent, splendid, full of hope. If you knew how much I've missed her here in Paris—I almost didn't leave, so I could keep on—but when that man Martin showed me her—I was so happy, knowing she existed."

"What do you mean, existed?"

"She was alive. The Nazis could have . . ."

"And how do you know that she didn't become a Nazi herself, Max?"

"That's impossible."

"She says her father's got an important post."

"You think a Nazi would go around giving cameras to vagabond kids so they could make portraits of their dreams?"

"That could be a front."

"You might as well accuse me of being a Nazi."

"Well, maybe you are, Max. Maybe we will."

"But for now just answer this: When you invited her to Paris, you had no way of knowing what she was up to, no way of knowing what she'd done in the years since you last saw her, right?"

"I had no need to know."

"Because you wanted to crawl into bed with her, Max. Come on, we're your friends, you can tell us the truth."

"Yes. I wanted to get into bed with her."

"Good. Our Max is beginning to tell us the truth. So you started planning how to bring her here, huh? All this bullshit about the Gestapo, nothing to it, right?"

"What I've said about the Gestapo is true. She's really in danger."

"You're saying it so we won't return her to Germany. So you can keep her here."

"She won't even talk to me, so . . . All I want now is to save her. So many people are going to die in the years to come. If we can save even one of them . . ."

"And where did you get the money, Max?"

"The same friend who—"

"Sure, sure, who told you they were out to kill your little lady—the one who went back to Germany?"

"Yes."

"And you spent the whole kit and caboodle on her?"

"Yes."

"And even with that heavy investment, you didn't get to fuck her, Max?"

"No."

"At least you must have masturbated while you had her on the phone, right?"

"No."

"But nine hours. What were you doing while you were buttering her up over the phone?"

"I slowly introduced myself into her life, getting her to know me. That's why I needed nine hours."

"And not because you had to get her ready for her work as a spy."

"You people are professional, and—"

"Thank you."

"—and you know that the Germans would never send a person to spy and contact a man who's an exile—"

"A Communist who says he's an exile, that is."

"Now you're going to tell me you don't believe I'm an exile?"

"Why did you leave your country, Max?"

"Yes, Max, that's something that's been puzzling me. Because I'll tell you that I would never leave France—I couldn't live far from my native land."

"Maybe Max has an explanation. Is it because Jews and Communists don't believe in a Fatherland, in loyalty to a country?"

"Is that why you left, Max?"

"I left because they would have killed me. Just like you would have left if you had—"

"We're no cowards."

"We wouldn't have left."

"And if the Nazis take over France?"

"Defeatists, you see what I was telling you. These guys are defeatists."

"You said it and you were right when you said it."

"We want you to know, Max, that the Nazis are never going to take over our land. And you know why?"

"Because we're here, watching, making sure the land is clean and healthy, without agitators and spies, without foreigners to contaminate us."

"And that's why we—do you know what we're going to do with you, Max?"

"You're going to release me."

"You've got a great sense of humor, Max."

"Max, Max. You must have guessed by now that we're sending you back to Germany, you must have known that's what we'd do with you."

"You're sending me to my death."

"Don't get melodramatic with us, Max."

"Yeah, you've got nothing to fear. Hitler's going to greet you with open arms. Now that he's such a buddy with Stalin."

"And her? What are you going to do with her?"

"Send her back along with you."

"Not her. Send me back, but don't—"

"But she's the one who wants to go back, Max."

"And if I could convince her that—"

"She says she doesn't want to talk to you."

"But maybe when you're both snugly back in Germany, she'll soften a bit. Or on the trip."

"Please don't send her back, please don't—"

"Hey, Max, we have to do our duty. We can't risk people like you smuggling information to the enemy—it's with intelligence that this war is going to be won or lost. We've just declared war, you know, in the National Assembly. Even the Communists voted for war."

"But not for long. Because in a couple of days' time they'll be illegal, Max—and we're going to hit them hard, Max, and when that happens you'll be glad to be back with your own countrymen . . ."

"But I don't see Max exactly grateful."

"And here we were thinking you'd be thanking us."

"Because another alternative was to execute you both, you and her, as spies, right?"

"Of course, our Max may not be grateful, because he doesn't know yet that we have a present for him."

"A birthday present. Because yesterday was your birthday and nobody celebrated it with you."

"So no one can say we haven't got a helluva heart."

"So no one can complain about our hospitality."

"We were thinking as you hadn't quite scored with your Barbara—"

"You didn't manage to give her a good fucking."

"We thought you might want to have us bring you your wife, Claudia, right?"

"Because we don't like to separate families. When the man in the family goes on a trip, we want the little wife to come along."

"You already went to get my wife?"

"Not yet, Max. We're just waiting for the green light from the Chief here to go and get you your birthday present, so all three of you can journey back to your country together. Just waiting for the Chief's signal."

There was a long pause and then they heard the other voice, the voice of the third man, the one who had remained silent, the man they call the Chief.

"Maybe that won't be necessary," says that voice.

"Maybe Max has something else he wants to tell us. Am I right, Max?"

For a long while, none of the men say a word, waiting for the reply. Finally, it comes:

"Yes. I was just thinking, sir, that maybe we could reach an agreement."

"Maybe, Max. But, of course, before we reach an agreement you'd have to tell us the truth."

"Yes. It may be time, sir, that I finally told you the truth."

"About the girl?"

"Yes, about the girl."

"That would be a good start, Max."

"And if I cooperate . . ."

"Maybe we can do you a favor."

"There's only one favor I'm interested in, sir."

"You want to save your little Barbara and your wife, is that it?"

"Yes, sir."

"And that's all?"

"One more thing."

"Yes. I've been thinking that maybe you'd like to see your Barbara one last time," says the voice of the man they call the Chief. "Maybe you'd like to spend some hours alone with her before you take that trip back to Germany. Is that what you'd like, Max?"

"Yes," says the voice of the man they call Max.

Now that the ending is near, now that the identity of that man may begin to emerge from the shadows, now that they have taken Max away and you cannot track him, now that Max is closing his mind down to you because you abandoned him, now is the time to start to wonder if you may not have been asking the wrong question.

Over and over, you have asked how Max can save Susanna.

But who is Susanna? What if she really had been a member of the resistance all this time? Why have you sought no access to her mind, her heart, her past? Why have you accepted to know her only through Max's eyes? Why do you automatically suppose she needs to be saved by somebody else? That she doesn't know what's good for her?

Wouldn't the right question be, have been: How can Susanna save herself?

It is a question that is being asked far too late.

It is too late to find Susanna. When they were separated at the police station, you chose to follow him, just as some time ago it was your instinctive choice to listen to his voice rather than hers. Now you cannot fathom where they have taken her.

It is a question Max must be asking himself, might know the answer to.

But you cannot find him.

He is defenseless in a dark place, he speaks in whispers, he moves slowly so no one can see him.

He hides.

He trusts no one.

He has a last story to tell, but no one can hear it.

"They're waiting for you upstairs," the concierge says, and he watches Claudia as if she didn't exist, watches Claudia as what she is: a woman who has no escape, a woman who has no one to offer her refuge in this world, a woman whose friends are all in prison or underground or running.

It is a look that is already calculating how much to ask a new tenant for the right to use Claudia's apartment, which will soon be vacant.

And yet, even as she laboriously goes up the stairs, Claudia allows herself to forget that look of naked avarice, she allows herself to pretend it isn't the police waiting for her upstairs, but Max, it has to be Max, who has returned to keep his promise that he will care for her if there is an emergency.

Her hope is absurd.

But it persists. Even when she finds the door open and presages that breathing, alien presence in her home, even when she finally sees that intruder who is undoubtedly an agent of some sort sitting at her kitchen table as if he were the owner, even then Claudia does not lose hope that everything will work out, because now the man stands up courteously and smiles at her, almost timidly. For a moment, the man says nothing. She sees that in his hands he has her photograph, the one Max always carries in his wallet.

"Claudia."

"Yes. I'm Claudia. And you are . . . ?"

The man waits for another instant, looking at her intensely.

"Michel Bernard," he finally says, without offering his hand. "From the French Sûreté. I'm here on behalf of your husband."

"Max is . . ."

"Alive."

"Something happened to—?"

"Please sit down, Claudia. If you don't mind, I'll call you Claudia. I have a couple of—messages, let's call them—messages to give you."

"From Max?"

"Please sit down."

Claudia sits down.

"I want to begin by assuring you that we are not going to arrest you. That's not the reason I've come here today. I want to assure you that I do not have the slightest intention of harming you."

Claudia says nothing.

"You thought I'd be coming for that, didn't you, to arrest you?"

"All my compatriots who were refugees here have been arrested, so I thought . . ."

"Almost all of them, yes."

"I thought there was no reason why I would be an exception."

"Oh, but there is a reason, there is, indeed."

"I don't see why."

"And if I were to say that your husband's the reason?"

"What happened to my husband?"

"Before I continue, I hope you understand that what I am going to tell you must be kept strictly confidential."

"We've been fighting Hitler for years. It's insulting that we shouldn't be trusted."

"We trust you. Precisely the point. That's why you have not been interned like so many others . . ."

"Where is Max?"

"He asked me to explain to you . . ."

"Where is he?"

"On his way back to Germany."

"It can't be true."

"He's been deported by our government."

"You're sending him back, you're—?"

"Serious charges had been leveled against him."

"What sort of charges?"

"Spying."

"That's absurd. You can't possibly believe that he—"

"In fact, I don't believe it. But I am not the only one working in my section."

"You interrogated him?"

"My subordinates. But I was present."

"You—did you hurt him, did you . . . ?"

"Nothing physical, Claudia. A couple of questions, a little bit of pressure, to see if we could get him to cooperate."

"Cooperate how?"

"We wanted your husband to go back to Germany of his own free will, to work for us, to send us information."

"And where's he going to get information to send you?"

"He says he's got contacts."

"And you believe him."

"I believe him, yes."

"This is crazy . . . that you, that he . . . The Nazis are going to kill him, they'll . . ."

"It's what he said, at first. But we think they won't. Of course, if he arrives back there screaming obscenities against Goebbels, they'll pack him off to a concentration camp right away, or maybe a quick bullet—but this is a very special moment for Germany, a time of confusion. Now that Hitler and Stalin have signed this pact, it wouldn't seem that strange that an exile should decide to put himself at his country's service in its war against the capitalist countries, now, would it?"

"Max would never . . ."

"If he wants to survive, he'll play the game . . . Imagine the scene: we give the Germans a man we accuse of espionage, whom we've decided to expel, and that man offers his services to the Third Reich. I think they'll receive him with open arms."

"And why should the Nazis believe him?"

"You'll recognize that your husband is—well, I'd call him a special sort of man."

"I don't know what you're talking about."

"He's a man whom one immediately believes, a man who always seems to be telling the truth, even if you've just heard him spew out the most incredible lie, you still believe what he's telling you. If you knew how difficult it was for us, I mean, before we got the truth from him, I don't want to tell you how difficult it was, because each time he kept inventing another story, and they were all so convincing. Do you know what I'm talking about?"

"Yes."

"But what I was getting at is that your husband talks and talks some more and we tend to believe him. And if he can do it with us—and with you, then why—"

"He's never lied to me!"

"If he's successful with everybody else, why not with them? And, after all, we won't lose anything by accepting his offer. Because if he's wrong, he's the one who's going to be in trouble. And as he asked us for so little, well, we decided to—"

"What did he ask for?"

"Two things. In fact, next to nothing. The first was your safety, Claudia, that we should let you live here unmolested—which, to tell you the truth, is also convenient for us, as your presence here guarantees that he'll go on cooperating."

"How do I know that what you're saying is true, how can I tell if you are who you say you are?"

"I've got a witness with me, ma'am, if you need someone to—"

"Who?"

"Do you remember that there was a second thing your husband wanted, another person he wanted to save . . . ?"

"Who? Who are you talking about?"

"If you go to your bedroom, Claudia, you will find, sleeping on your bed, a young woman called Barbara."

"I don't understand."

"She's your husband's daughter."

"We haven't got a daughter."

"I said, your husband's."

"He hasn't got a daughter."

"You don't know about it and he asks you to forgive him for not having told you before. He didn't want to cause you pain."

"He's never hidden anything from me. This isn't—"

"The young woman was conceived in a brief love affair he had before he met you, that's what he asked me to tell you—that you shouldn't reproach him for it. He was very young—seventeen, I think he said he was when—"

"I don't believe it. I can't believe it. He's been in touch with her all these years?"

"He says no, that he hasn't, that when a young German student whom he ran into one day at a café here in Paris, when that young man talked to him about a girlfriend back in Berlin and showed him a photograph, he recognized his daughter immediately. It's a long story, but he decided to bring her to Paris in order to . . ."

"In order to what?"

"He says to save her. But there was a little problem. She didn't want to stay."

"She wanted to return to Germany?"

"Yes."

"And how did he convince her to stay?"

"Nobody convinced her. We carried out his plan: when we deported him, we refused to hand her over to the Germans. It wasn't easy. We had to use force, drug her."

"And tomorrow, when she wakes, who can stop her from going back on her own, if she's so eager to—?"

"She won't be able to. That's what Max asked us to make sure of—we told the German Embassy staff that we had received definitive information that this young woman was decidedly anti-Nazi and that we could not put her in danger by deporting her—and that thanks to her we had been able to arrest two German agents who had dared to murder a French citizen called Antoinette Severet a few weeks ago."

"You arrested them? That's a relief. And she's really the one who . . . ?"

"Your husband's the one who told us where to

find them. He knew all about them. You can see that our collaboration has gotten off to a good start."

"Max told me that he suspected they were French policemen."

"He probably told you that so as not to disturb you. They were German agents."

"And that poor girl, the Nazis believe she's responsible for—and it's not true."

"What's true is what people want to believe is true, Claudia. And this maneuver guarantees that, whatever the truth may be, your government thinks this young woman Barbara is an opponent of the regime. That's what Max wanted: to ensure that his daughter could not go back."

"His daughter! He never wanted children. How could he—?"

"Men lie to the women they fall in love with, Claudia. They're scared that if they tell them about the past . . ."

"And what does his—daughter think about all this?"

"I imagine she's not too happy."

"And what am I supposed to tell her when she wakes up?"

"Most important is that you never tell her that Max is her father. She doesn't know it and your husband would rather that she never find out that he sacrificed his life for her. He already said goodbye to her. We gave them some time alone so they could . . ."

"And what role do I play in all this?"

"Well, as you can see, your husband has sent her to you."

"Why me?"

"He said you would understand."

"He said that? That I would understand?"

"Yes. He said there was no other person in the world to care for her and that you would understand."

"And how am I supposed to contact him?"

"I'm going to be your contact person."

"You'll bring me messages from him?"

"Whenever I can."

"And if you lose the war . . ."

"I will help you, ma'am. I promised your husband that I would help you both to escape. But there will be no need. We are not going to lose the—"

"And you—why are you doing this? Acting as messenger."

"It's nothing special. It's part of my agreement with him, with Max."

"That's not true. I know about these things, Mr. . . ."

"Don't mister me, please. Bernard, Michel Bernard. I prefer you don't call me mister."

"I know about these things. You seem to be going out of your way to save us."

"There are many people I'm trying to save, Claudia."

"Germans?"

"That's as much as I can tell you."

"I need to know. I need you to tell me why you have this special preoccupation with two women who . . ."

"Your husband told me you were—different, that sometimes you could—read people's thoughts. You can't read mine?"

"Max is always exaggerating. You can see he's wrong: I never guessed that he had a daughter. If she is his daughter. That's almost . . . I still can't believe it."

"Max said to trust him. As you always have."

"As I always have. Though he lied to me about this."

"We all have some secret nobody else knows."

The man stands up slowly, puts the chair back where he found it, in the exact position as before he sat down. Claudia stops him with a gesture.

"And your secret . . . ?"

"I really must be going, Claudia."

"And when are you coming back?"

"As soon as I hear from Max."

"You're in charge of him?"

"Yes."

"So he's in your hands?"

"Yes."

"I need to know, Michel, I need to understand why you're doing this, why you want to protect us . . ."

"Why do you need to know?"

"I need to know if I can trust you."

"You can trust me."

"But you can't trust me? You can't tell me what it is you're hiding?"

"It's not something I can speak about."

"Well, maybe it's time you started."

"I'll see you next week, Claudia."

"No, no—you can't leave until you—"

"I'll bring news from Max."

She lets time go by slowly, measuring him, looking into his eyes. Finally, she speaks:

"Do whatever you have to do."

"May I ask you for a favor before I leave?"

"There's no harm in asking."

"If you could speak to me without that anger in your voice. It doesn't suit you."

She hesitates. Then:

"I'll do what I can."

"One more thing. Can I tell Max that you'll take care of that young woman?"

"As if she were my own daughter," Claudia says.

Is that all?

Is this how the story ends?

Without one more word from him? With his voice swallowed by the fog, swallowed by the night? His voice and so many other voices?

How do we contact those who, dead or alive, leave no trace?

Is this how their story ends?

With Max as a victim at best, or a traitor at worst?

Or can we remain loyal to him—now, at this last moment—can we find a way of connecting with him for one last flicker, listen to the words of that man who died many years ago in that country whose language you do not know, transcribe one final hour of words uttered by that man who once trusted you.

Many will think that you are also making all this up, again compensating for not having been able to help him, again looking for a way to write one story that has a good, decent man at its core.

But who is to say that Max, as I hear him now, across time and death and language, did not call to me from a moment before my birth, who is to say he did not exist as we have dreamt him?

Who can swear that my brother Max did not really speak these final words to us in the deepening night?

You must forgive me, Susanna, for breaking my promise, for making you come to my dreams against your will.

I can assure you it is the last time.

You do not answer me.

I suspected that you wouldn't. Which doesn't make your silence hurt me less. But then you were the one who explained to me, so many years ago, when you began visiting me the first time, that the pain of things, my child, does not diminish because you understand them.

I already told you through Michel Bernard in a letter, but I want you to know directly from me that I did not betray you. That is the version you and anybody else who heard this story would end up believing. But everything I did, you've got to believe me, I did to save you. If I had let you go back to Germany, if I hadn't made a deal with the French so they wouldn't hand you over, you'd be dead right now. Or, like us, waiting for death. And I'd rather not mention how they would have worked over your beautiful body, what these bastards would have done with that beautiful body I was able to touch for a few hours, that I was able to recognize and celebrate during those hours that now seem almost nonexistent—there in that prison cell in Paris where they brought you so I could say goodbye. But what matters most: your daughter would not have been born. Yes, I know that you have a daughter and that her name is Victoria. Martin told me all about it when they brought him here this morning, more dead than alive. That's why I need you to come and visit me one last time.

I know that wasn't what I agreed to. I know that I promised that if you gave me that one night I would leave you free forever, that I would never again ask you for anything, not even to recall you to my dreams. I think that it was that final offer which convinced you, there in that deep darkness of a French prison cell. "Are you really ready," you asked, a shadow inside the shadows, "to sacrifice all the hours of your future dreams?"

"All of them," I answered. "But it may not be that much of a sacrifice. I haven't got that much to live."

And now you can see that I was right.

Take my hand, Susanna, that's it, take this hand which that night you guided toward the buttons of your blouse as you had so often done in my dreams, take my hand and follow me. We don't have much time. I don't know how long I can stay asleep. Loom over, onto the other side of my closed eyes, and there you will see me, in a corner of this cellar where they've locked my sad body away. You can see that I am the only one sleeping. The other prisoners condemned to die, and especially Martin, cannot believe that I would want to or even could go to sleep when there is so little left till dawn and those footsteps in the corridor and those men who are going to execute us. Can you see Martin there? Can you see him with Victoria's photograph clutched in his hand? Now that he thinks I can't see him, look how he smiles at that picture you sent him, listen to how he murmurs the silly things that a man might say to a daughter he never saw born and whom he will never see grow up, devouring the photo as if he were trying to stuff that little girl deeper than his eyes, as if he were trying to make sure that she will accompany him from inside when the moment to face the firing squad arrives, that she will give him strength when they come for him.

It was because of her existence that I had to contact you. I need to know, Susanna, if Victoria was conceived that night we spent together in France. Or if you were already carrying her, fathered by Martin in your last lovemaking with him in Berlin before he left, if she was already growing inside you when you were generous to a man who had loved you for twenty-five years, so that he would not die without having known what the inside of your body was like?

Is it possible that she is my daughter?

I know that she was very small when she was born—so small, according to Martin, that she almost did not survive your hasty flight from Paris when the city fell to Hitler, so small that she could have been a seven-month-old baby at birth, she could have been born before her time, like so many things of mine that never seem to come out right. But I'm not going to dwell on what has gone wrong, how badly things have turned out for us: you called your daughter Victoria—and I like that name, I like your having named her Victoria precisely as a way of embodying your faith in some sort of future triumph at the very moment in which defeat was everywhere and the Nazi armies were advancing on Paris. I want to think that we are someday going to win this war and that maybe in that future other men and other women will be able to build a world where there will be no more cellars like this one, walls like those that bar our escape right now. Because I cannot stop asking myself if we had been born at another time, a time without wars or misery or fear or concentration camps, I cannot stop asking myself if perhaps everything would not have been different. Or is it inevitable that this last scene between you and me be repeated over and over and over again through the centuries every time someone like me dreams someone like you? Or could it be that our misfortune does not depend on the time when we were born but rather in what particular body we happen to inhabit in that time, what destiny we were given to live, what power we had at our fingertips, how ready we were to use that power?

If I had been born French, like Michel Bernard, if I had been like him a high-ranking officer in French Intelligence, if I had come across your photograph when I was interrogating a German resistance fighter—then this story would be different. Then I would be the one who, like Michel Bernard right now, is seducing that woman. I would be the one giving that woman and the woman they call Barbara and Barbara's daughter, I would be the one to give them protection, I would have arranged their escape from Paris when the Nazis took the city, I would be next to you now in the South of France, waiting to leave for the other side of the ocean. I don't know if Michel Bernard dreamt of Claudia before he saw her, as I dreamt you; or if he fell in love with her when he saw her photo in that interrogation room; or if he knew her from before, if he had crossed her path one splendid Parisian day and from that moment on began watching us, waiting for his chance over the years, and organized everything so he could possess her without her ever knowing what he was doing, arranged our arrest in Paris and my own arrest here in Berlin and even perhaps Antoinette's death and before that the death of my men in Germany; or if all this is no more than another of Scheherazade's stories that I entertain myself with in the darkness of this cellar where I have spent the last months. The truth is that now he loves her—and because he loves her he will harbor you and your daughter—and when all too soon the news of my execution comes he will marry the woman who was once my wife. The truth is that, except for that one night, I was not given more than a dream. Like most of humanity, most of the men and women who have lived on this earth. But I should not complain. At least I was offered the privilege of this dream in which I speak to you, this dream in which you do not answer me, this dream in which I compare your mouth which does not smile back at me with Victoria's mouth in the photograph.

If I had been able to identify my mouth in her mouth when Martin passed me the photograph, my eyes in her eyes, any trait that would have assured me that I might be that child's father—believe me, I would never have brought you here. But under the suppressed light of this cellar, the picture did not answer any of my questions—and Martin's presence by my side as I digested the photograph forced me, in spite of my own desire, to find in the girl those high cheeks of Martin's, perhaps his nose, a vague familiarity.

And of course, with time, Victoria will start looking more and more like Martin. When, within a few years, the girl is old enough to look at herself in the mirror and can begin to interrogate her face in search of her father's features, she will discover Martin's, because that is whom she will be seeking, he is the designated progenitor, the legendary father Claudia and Michel Bernard will speak of when she comes to them for stories. Or will Victoria ever glimpse, watching her from inside and behind her own eyes, those eyes of her Uncle Max, the forgotten first husband of her Aunt Claudia, the uncle who died in Germany alongside her father a few months after she was born? Maybe she'll have seen me in the photo which I hope not only Claudia has on her night table, the photo which I hope you have also put there, next to your bed. The photo which may be able to speak to Victoria.

Because you believe that photographs know how to speak.

Or so you said that one night when you finally kept the promise you made when I turned twelve, that unreal night in France when you allowed me to enter you as you had been entering me during twenty-five years, that night you recounted to me things about your life that you had never told me before in dreams nor told Martin either and that he therefore was never able to transmit to me. You had the photos of your ten boys in your bag, and though it was too dark to distinguish the images, you passed them to me one by one so my fingers could acknowledge them—and you told me, vaguely caressing my hair, that when we'd arrive in Berlin I had to come and see the rest of the photographs and also the kids, the first sign that perhaps you imagined me as part of your future. I knew, of course, that you would never see those children again and I suspected that I would not find them—and the only thing I've been able to do, Susanna, is send you some of the photos I managed to rescue from that house in which you lived with them and which the Gestapo raided and plundered. That night I did not speak to you about that, about what was coming. I preferred to point out, murmuring, that you were repeating with those boys of twelve the same gesture of sanctuary you had offered me in my dreams and at exactly the same age. And I thought, but did not mention, how strange that you had been unable to save me with all your advice and that now you would also be unable to save them, nobody, nothing could save those boys who dared to dream in a world of murderers.

But you did not anticipate this in that blurred French night, and it was then that you explained to me your theory about photographs—that some photographs know how to speak. It was your mother who had told you this when you were small, and for years you thought that it just happened to be your bad luck that the photos would quiet down when you were present and you were sure that they were only waiting for you to leave the room to reveal their secrets. At times you would try to become completely invisible to see if you could fool the damn photos, stealthily put your ear to the door of the closed room in the hope of trapping their conversation. It was then that you must have sworn that you'd be a photographer yourself when you grew up—but that you wouldn't keep the secret of the photos to yourself as your mother and the other adults had done, that you would spread your knowledge throughout the world, you were going to give other children the means to take snapshots of their dreams, so their dreams could speak.

And now that those children are no longer with you and I am not there, will you say the same things to your daughter? Will you tell her that some photos speak? Will you teach her patiently the questions one must ask of a photograph so it can reveal its hidden life?

And what is really essential, Susanna: if someday the withered image of the man who died so many years ago and who has no one else but that photo to speak for him, if the day comes when my picture begins to suggest to your daughter this story of mine which only you know, what will you do? If I manage to find a way into Victoria's dreams as you found a way into mine and I murmur a few phrases? What will you do? Will you shut the door to the room where the photos your Berlin kids took are watching you from the walls and then make Victoria swear that she will never tell her Aunt Claudia, that she must swear she will never breathe one word to her aunt or anyone else—and then you will tell her how one day you entered a hotel room in Paris, and who was calling you, who had been calling you since before your birth? Or will you tell her that she's imagining things? That it's not true that photos speak? Will you tell her that dreams lie?

That's why I asked you to come and see me tonight. To ask you one last favor in this last dream of my life.

I am about to awaken. I can feel at the other side of reality someone shaking my shoulder. You're already leaving, you're leaving. It doesn't matter that you did not speak to me. You can go, Susanna, without telling me if I am the father of that girl. I do not need to know. When I open my eyes, I will find my friend Martin by my side. He will help me up from the soiled floor where I last made contact with you. Of this dream, and all the other dreams, I will tell him nothing. He would feel betrayed by people he admires and loves—and that wondrous faith in humanity that he showed at our first meeting in Paris has been slowly eroding under the certainty that someone sold us out, sold him, sold me, someone we believed in gave our names to the enemy. It would be a crime to steal from Martin that faith which he still has, that faith which keeps on shouting silently from inside him that the world does not have to be the way it is. He needs that faith to face what we will both have to face all too soon. That is what he needs.

As for me, what I need is no more than a gesture from you. I have no one else in the world to turn to. If you could indicate, even if indirectly, that the day when your daughter comes to ask about her past, you will tell her the story of the night she was created, the night when her mother and her father started the universe for her, if you could . . . I only need something slight from you: press my hand as a way of saying goodbye, tell me with your hand in my hand that is leaving and awakening, tell me you will not deny Victoria that story I can no longer tell alone, the story which can no longer exist without your words.

Or will you allow our history to die with me?

Acknowledgments

All books, and especially this one, owe their existence to many voices that encourage and inspire their supposed author.

This novel is already dedicated, like so many of my books, to Angélica, the primary reader of my life and my work, but there are others that should not be forgotten.

First of all, my oldest son, Rodrigo, with whom I talked this novel over incessantly, on long walks, until one day he asked me the essential question, clear and simple, that would end up giving me my bearings as I tried to make sense of the story that was being born. Nor would this book be possible without the constant company of my younger son, Joaquín, who asked and still asks other sorts of questions.

Konfidenz could not exist in its present state were it not for the enthusiasm, care, and intelligence of my two editors, one working with my Spanish text and the other with my text in English, both of whom, by an extraordinary coincidence, have the same first name: John Glusman, of Farrar, Straus and Giroux, and Juan Forn, of Planeta Argentina.

Thanks as well to Margaret Lawless, my loyal, cheerful, and

efficient assistant, and to the staff, professors, and students of Duke University, who nurtured my life in many different ways as I struggled with *Konfidenz*. And to Deborah Karl, Bridget Love, and Raquel de la Concha, my agents, who defended this project with steadfast ferocity at a time when support was truly needed.

Finally, many others made crucial contributions to this book: the superb photographer, Wendy Ewald; our friends Jon Beller and Neferti Tadiar; Professor Alice Kaplan; and, unknowingly, my friend Peter Gabriel.

All of you, each in your own way, helped me to understand the deeper history which, in spite of my own desire and certainly theirs, the not so imaginary protagonists of *Konfidenz* have had to live.

ALSO AVAILABLE FROM

Vintage Español / Alfaguara

The Spanish-language edition of

KONFIDENZ

ISBN: 0-679-76333-3